T0124294

MAN
-TO-
MAN
PLEASURE

A Collection of Homoerotic Short Stories

Paul-François Sylvestre

MAN -TO- MAN PLEASURE
A COLLECTION OF HOMOEROTIC SHORT STORIES

Copyright © 2020 Paul-François Sylvestre.

All rights reserved. No part of this book may be used or reproduced by any means, graphic, electronic, or mechanical, including photocopying, recording, taping or by any information storage retrieval system without the written permission of the author except in the case of brief quotations embodied in critical articles and reviews.

This is a work of fiction. All of the characters, names, incidents, organizations, and dialogue in this novel are either the products of the author's imagination or are used fictitiously.

iUniverse books may be ordered through booksellers or by contacting:

iUniverse
1663 Liberty Drive
Bloomington, IN 47403
www.iuniverse.com
1-800-Authors (1-800-288-4677)

Because of the dynamic nature of the internet, any web addresses or links contained in this book may have changed since publication and may no longer be valid. The views expressed in this work are solely those of the author and do not necessarily reflect the views of the publisher, and the publisher hereby disclaims any responsibility for them.

Any people depicted in stock imagery provided by Getty Images are models, and such images are being used for illustrative purposes only. Certain stock imagery © Getty Images.

ISBN: 978-1-5320-8360-0 (sc)
ISBN: 978-1-5320-8361-7 (e)

Library of Congress Control Number: 2019921184

Print information available on the last page.

iUniverse rev. date: 01/10/2020

Contents

Introduction

I'm a seventy-two-year-old French-Canadian author living in Toronto. All of my fifty books have been published in French, some in the province of Québec, most in Ontario. My first book was a diary of my coming out in 1976; since then four novels, two essays, two poetry books, and one collection of short stories with gay content have joined it.

In early 2019, I joined an international online dating service called Silver Daddies and began corresponding with younger guys interested in meeting older men. Some were from the United States, and others were from England, Russia, Iran, Ivory Coast, and Bangladesh. My email exchanges with these correspondents in their twenties to midthirties brought me to writing personalized short stories in English, my second language.

Interested in sharing some of these autofiction texts, I discovered that a Swedish site called Gay Demon had been publishing porn stories since 2006, at a rate of about 1,200 per year. I sent my first story—about a Bangladeshi cyclist—on April 18, 2019, and it was put online the next day.

All of the stories included in this book have appeared on the Gay Demon site, free of charge and copyright. They are grouped under six headings: "First Time and Coming Out," "Interracial," "Daddies," "Russian and Ukrainian File," "American File," and "Bondage and Group Sex."

I hope you enjoy these man-to-man pleasures in words, the first step to the real thing!

Paul-François Sylvestre

1

First Time and Coming Out

1.1 On the Bicycle Path

As Paul was bicycling one morning, just as the sun rose through the clouds, he crossed paths with a young cyclist in an orange shirt and tight black shorts. They both smiled and continued on their ways—only to find that the bicycle path wound around in such a way that they crossed again and again, with bigger smiles each time.

Paul thought, *This cyclist is so cute. How can I approach him? How can I seduce him?* Finally he got an idea. He climbed off his bicycle, sat on the ground next to the path, and began massaging his leg as if he had a cramp. As the young cyclist approached him again, Paul winked and waved his hand nonchalantly.

This was enough to catch the attention of the handsome dude, who immediately stopped to see if everything was okay. "Hi there. Did you have an accident?"

"No, just a light cramp." *A white lie*, Paul thought. "Nice of you to inquire. What's your name?"

"I'm Jony. And you?"

"Paul. You're in great shape. That's a very athletic body."

"Thanks. I can give you a massage if you want," Jony offered.

"That would certainly energize me, Jony."

They moved toward a grassy area, and Paul let Jony's hands do the work. To encourage him and send a message, Paul gave him a pat on the buns. Jony brushed lightly against his "patient." There was excitement in the air.

"Can you massage my thighs also?" Paul asked. "I feel some tension there."

Jony replied, "No problem. They seem pretty firm to me."

"Your hands have a magic touch, and your smile is inviting."

"What do you mean?"

"Can I thank you with a kiss?" asked Paul

"Hmm, I've never been kissed by a man."

"But I think you'd like it. Am I right?"

"I guess so," Jony said.

Not wasting one second, Paul embraced Jony—softly at first, then more passionately. The close, wet contact triggered a bulge in each cyclist's crotch. Paul pulled Jony closer to exert cock-to-cock pressure. "Feels good, hey, Jony?"

Jony answered with a moan of pleasure.

Paul said, "We can bicycle to my place, Jony. The least

I can do is offer you a glass of lemonade—or something more, if you want."

"That would be nice," Jony agreed. "I think I can learn a lot from a mature man like you."

In no time, Paul and Jony were comfortably installed in a love seat, cuddling and kissing with frenzy. Paul kneaded Jony's muscled pectorals and biceps, gradually moving to his firm ass and slowly undressing the radiant dark-skinned cyclist.

Jony's reaction was instinctive as his hard cock jolted in Paul's face, begging for a caress.

"Let's go to my bedroom," Paul suggested. "We'll be more comfortable there."

"Is your bed like a wrestling ring?" asked Jony.

"I see that you have something kinky in mind."

"I'm so aroused," Jony replied. "It's my first time with a man."

"You will not regret it, believe me."

Once on the bed, the two cyclists became nude wrestlers. Paul applied a bit of oil to give Jony's adorable body a sparkling shine, and to make him slide even more into Paul's arms. They quickly ended up in the sixty-nine position, sucking each other's cock with appetite.

Feeling that Jony was on the verge of cumming, Paul stopped abruptly. "Don't cum now. The best is yet to come."

Jony asked, "What do you mean?"

"I want to rim you."

"What's that?"

Paul didn't explain in words. He just slid his tongue down Jony's cock, balls, and ass crack to reach the anus. "In French, we call this the *rosette*, or rosebud," said Paul just before he darted Jony's asshole in a frenzy. Initiated into rimming, the cute young cyclist was ready to explode, but Paul exclaimed, "Wait, I want to drink your nectar!"

Back in the sixty-nine position, both Paul and Jony had a succulent milky drink—100 percent homogenized, 100 percent homo.

Jony was no longer a virgin to sex with a man. He now dreamed of becoming Paul's partner, on the bicycle path and on the erotic road, maybe even on the highway to love.

1.2   Man-to-Man "Brief" Pleasure

Tom had an older sister, a twin sister, and a younger sister, but no brother with whom to cuddle. He had seen his daddy in boxer shorts only once, lying flat on his belly with one hairy ball hanging out. Tom was eleven or twelve years old when he first saw another boy in underwear. In fact, he got to see two for the price of one.

His school in Northern Ontario, Canada, did not offer a physical education course, so boys never undressed in front of one another. One day, Tom, Dick, and Harry got into a garage and decided to drop their pants and expose their underwear. Tom was wearing boxer shorts, whereas Dick and Harry were wearing briefs: one in Fruit of the Loom, and the other in Hugo Boss. Tom was surprised that there were different types of underwear and that white briefs kind of aroused him. Needless to say, he explained to his mother that he was old enough to choose the kind of underwear he wanted; she agreed to scrap his "sexless" boxers—as Tom would later call them—and replaced them with white briefs.

Tom got an opportunity to examine a variety of briefs when he became a teenager, passing from twelve to thirteen. He attended an all-boys school, and a medical examination was scheduled. Every guy had to strip to his underwear. Tom immediately spotted the guys in white undies and noticed that they were often fondling themselves. It seemed that sex games would always start by comparing each other's underwear. At that age, sexual experimentation could obviously lead to measuring each other's cock, both flaccid and erect, with a ruler.

Tom's father wanted his son to develop his biceps and tone his abdominal muscles to get a six-pack, so he enrolled Tom in the local gym club.

What a good idea! thought Tom. The young man could take his time in the locker room and scrutinize all the jocks in white briefs. Some of them removed their underwear to put on white jockstraps. Tom would stay behind, wait till everyone had gone to the gym, sneak into a locker, pull the smelly white undies out, and sniff it feverishly. Wow, the man perfume!

As Tom was finishing eleventh grade, new neighbors moved next door, and they had a son the same age as Tom. The two boys became close friends who couldn't seem to get close enough.

One day, Tom went to Jeff's place after school. Jeff's mother asked her son to change out of his school clothes. Heading toward the steps, Jeff turned around and asked

Tom, "Are you coming with me?" Fantasy was about to become reality.

As he entered his best friend's room and sat on the bed, Tom was excited because he knew that he would finally see Jeff in his underwear. Jeff shut and locked the door, removed his shirt, took off his shoes, and finally dropped his pants.

Tom exclaimed, "Wow, Jeff, you're wearing Fruit of the Loom briefs!"

"Of course," Jeff replied. "Do you like them?"

"You're damn sure. I have a strong fetish for white undies."

"Care to smell my crotch?" Jeff offered.

Heaven on earth!

Tom not only smelled Jeff's white undies, but also licked and drooled on his friend's clothed crotch with zeal. It was so fucking succulent! Tom maneuvered to reach Jeff's ass crack, searching for the small dirty spot he called the big jackpot. This "holy shit" was giving him the strongest hard-on he had ever experienced.

Jeff wanted his share of the cake, too, so he undressed his classmate. But he was aroused by guys in underpants as much Tom was, so he didn't remove Tom's Calvin Klein briefs. When his mother would get a clothes catalog in the mail, Jeff would secretly flip to the men's section and gaze at the display of briefs, caressing the pictures of white crotches and imagining what they were so angelically hiding.

Jeff and Tom rolled over on the bed, not knowing that their position was called sixty-nine, and started to rub their faces in each other's bulging angel cloth. Jeff stretched Tom's elastic band with his teeth, chewed the clothed balls, and kissed and licked the cock until it almost sneaked out of the wet white briefs. But the rule was to always keep the jewels tightly wrapped during the tongue and hand massages that inevitably triggered an explosion of nectar.

Tom's biggest reward was keeping Jeff's creamy undies as a souvenir of his first full-blown experience of man-to-man "brief" pleasure. Later, at barely twenty-six, he had a drawer filled with eight different brands of smelly white undies: Calvin Klein, Emporio Armani, Hugo Boss, Diesel, Polo Ralph Lauren, Derek Rose, Ermenegildo Zegna, and Dolce & Gabbana.

1.3 Shove It In, Shove It Out

William, a sixty-two-year-old teacher with a short white beard, has two months off in the summer and decides to drive from Toronto to the Rocky Mountains. He plans to visit a cousin in Winnipeg, Manitoba, and two nephews in Calgary, Alberta. The stretch across Saskatchewan between Winnipeg and Calgary will probably be uneventful, since fields of wheat and canola tend to get boring after a few hours. But William is in for a surprise …

The Trans-Canada Highway passes through Swift Current, Saskatchewan, where William stops to stretch his legs. As he pulls out of town, he sees a rainbow flag on the front porch of a wooden house, next to a welcome sign. He parks his car, walks up to the front door, and knocks.

A tall, slim guy in his early twenties appears, wearing a big smile. William will soon find out that Kurt, too, is a teacher. He's also an artist, and his work serves as a unique way of coming out to friends—and visitors such as William.

Kurt says, "You're probably driving to Jasper, Lake Louise, and Banff National Park, right?"

"Yes," answers William, "but a visit here could probably be more exciting. Am I right?"

"Of course! I can give you a hand. Just sit here next to me."

"Your living room is like an art gallery, full of intriguing homoerotic collages and structures," William says.

Kurt explains, "I tend to include fetish articles in my creations, like jockstraps, cock rings, dildos, and spanking paddles. I find it so arousing. Gets me horny."

"I can see that. Your crotch is bulging."

On that note, Kurt embraces William and kisses him lusciously. They cuddle, sip a beer, and take off their shirts. William shows off his hairy chest to an excited Kurt, who proposes a tour of his playroom.

As he gets up, William grasps the young teacher's butt, which is tightly wrapped in faded blue jeans. He's about to experience the best summer trip of his life. Forget nephews in Calgary and natural parks in Alberta—the fun is mainly in the Prairies.

The playroom occupies half the basement. A saddle solidly installed in the middle of the floor goes nicely with the leather chaps that Kurt wears on top of his jeans and a cowboy hat that adds a magic touch. William removes his shorts, showing a plentiful Cocksoc jockstrap. He invites Kurt to get down on his knees and present his rear end for a proper treatment. A narrow paddle in his hand, William aims for the stitched seam on his jeans, making Kurt moan with pleasure for an encore!

As a teacher, William pays attention to details, especially when he's stripping his partner. He smells the leather chaps, caresses the bulging denim crotch, removes the belt to swirl it around Kurt's neck, brings his partner to naked splendor, and installs him on the saddle. William kisses the huge pink mushroom and gradually swallows the cowboy's pistol, bringing it to the size of a bazooka.

"That feels good, but I want to be a perfect host," says Kurt. "I read your mind, and it begs for ass play."

"Damn right!" exclaims William. "You need a lunch break, so why not eat my rump roast?"

Kurt has never seen such a hairy rosebud amid a titillating sweaty aroma. He plunges his face into the inviting crack, licks it while slapping his partner's rear cheeks, then starts darting his tongue into the Cheerio.

"Shove it in, shove it out—rimming is divine," William cries out.

Kurt is pleased to oblige, but he also wants to role-play. He has cowboy cattle roping in mind, so he grabs a lasso and ties their bodies together. The horse in the stable section of the playroom is obviously Kurt. Hung like a stallion, he moves his partner to a bed, which is actually a bale of hay covered by an iconic Hudson Bay Company blanket, with its green, red, yellow, and indigo stripes on a white background.

William is ready to honor a young, zealous teacher equipped with a magic wand. His hungry ass is tight, but nothing is beyond Kurt's fucking know-how. William wonders if his partner has practiced on some jock student, like he did years ago.

To ensure a perfect and smooth penetration, Kurt opens a jar of Crisco, greases his thick dick, and gradually starts pounding William's satanic haven.

"Fuck! That feels so damn good," cries out the young teacher.

"Shove it in, shove it out! Bareback fucking is divine, but shoot your load in my face!" William cries.

Kurt reaches unprecedented heights in man-to-man pleasure. It is so intense that he invites William to spend the rest of his vacation in Swift Current … where the libido current passes swiftly.

1.4 Narcissus Dreams of Fucking Himself

airy men look like real men who have more important things to think about than waxing their ball bags. That's pretty much Amine's philosophy. Okay, he's a muscular twenty-eight-year-old Algerian guy with a V-shaped torso that displays a thick black rug. Amine goes to the gym and pumps iron five times a week, triggering compliments on his firm biceps and sculpted six-pack.

No one knows that Amine is gay, for the simple reason that homosexuality is prohibited by law in Algeria. The prevailing social attitude toward gays is openly negative, even violent. He's had sex with a few women, but he never found the experience to be entirely fulfilling—pun intended.

Amine dreams of kissing a man with a beard and sucking a dick as thick as his own weapon. In fact, his fantasy is to have sex with a look-alike, someone who reminds him of himself. Amine is the incarnation of Narcissus. Like the Greek hunter from Thespiae in

Boeotia, Amine is fixated on his own striking beauty and his physical appearance, especially his great *ass*ets.

One day he meets Omar, a twenty-five-year-old trainer at the gym. Omar is the same height, about six foot one, and roughly the same weight at 195 pounds. They work out together, and Amine can almost smell the furry pecs of the trainer on the bench press. He believes that hairiness helps increase a man's sexy scent. When they take showers at the same time, although at opposite ends of the tiled floor, Amine admires Omar's firm butt. The young trainer looks somewhat like Joe Manganiello, but without a beard.

"Do you want me to rub your back with soap?" asks Amine.

"That would be great," replies Omar. "Use a bit of pressure, like in a massage."

"Okay. You can reciprocate afterward, my friend."

The touching is firm but not erotic. Both men feel that the massage is done with a certain restraint. The two gym buddies, however, have a chance to glance at each other's crotch. They are a real mirror image: circumcised cock, 3.75 inches at rest, tight dumbbells, short pubic hair.

In the locker room, Amine offers to dry Omar's back and nonchalantly slides his hands across the trainer's furry pecs. He says, "You sure are a Mister Muscle, a real virile man. That's what I want to become."

Omar says, "I think you're already there, Amine, and you love what's in front of you. Am I right, Narcissus?"

"What do you mean? I don't understand the word *Narcis*—"

"Narcissus, a hunter in a Greek legend. You are hunting for a look-alike man."

Amine says, "Too bad you don't have a beard, Omar."

"In three weeks, I will be your reflection in the pool, not a mere white flower," Omar replies.

Omar and Amine meet regularly for gym practice, always getting closer but never grabbing each other firmly, barely engaging in discreet frottage. Hints while dressing or undressing in the locker room have paid off. Both now wear sleeveless yellow T-shirts, white jockstraps, black Speedo shorts, red Nike running shoes ... and short black beards. Narcissus is nearing the pool.

They wait until everyone has left the locker room before heading to the showers, their manhoods deliciously blooming to almost seven inches. If you had been there, dear reader, you would have seen identical twins kissing tenderly, squeezing each other's butts, caressing black velvet torsos, pressing a blood pudding ... until D-Day.

The battleground is the clean wet tile floor acting as the legendary Narcissus pool. Amine can finally suck a dick as long and thick as his own joystick. He can bite an incarnation of his round butt. He can rim a perfect image of his rosebud. He can give a golden shower to a look-alike face. He can fuck himself forever and ever!

Omar is now a shadow of Narcissus, strung up from head to toe, a puppet, *his* puppet, dancing to the tune of his vanity and the beat of his narcissism, always and constantly hypnotized. As the Austrian poet Rainer Maria Rilke once wrote, a man can be encircled by a pair of arms as by a shell "while forever he endures the outrage of his too pure image."

1.5 Coming Out in the Seventies

Born in a French Canadian, Catholic family, Maurice turned thirteen in 1960. As a teenager, he lived through the assassination of President John F. Kennedy and the death of Pope John XXIII. The 1960s were known as an era of sexual liberation, but Maurice was far removed from that revolution. Sex was never a topic of discussion with his parents, let alone in the classroom. His parents sent him to a seminary, not so much to become a priest as to follow a classical course leading to a bachelor's degree in philosophy.

During those eight years at seminary, Maurice lived more or less in an aseptic, if not sterile, bubble. No girlfriends, no pot, no wild parties. When he entered the workplace, Maurice was still a virgin. At twenty-three, he invited a female colleague to the National Arts Centre and played tennis with her. His secretary teased him by spreading the rumor of a possible engagement, but nothing could have been further from the truth.

There comes a time when the bubble has to burst,

when fantasies must seek to actualize themselves. In other words, Maurice was attracted to guys. Was he the only one like that in his community? He had heard some cousins talk of a "sissy" uncle, but he had no idea at that time what the word really meant. The truth was a blow: "I'm a sissy, a queer, a faggot, a homosexual."

Maurice had no idea how to actualize his sexual fantasy … until he came across a small ad in the newspaper: "Male escort. A guy will come over for one hour for sixty dollars. Call …"

After a week of dithering, Maurice finally dialed the infamous phone number and learned that the escort was indeed available the next day. Maurice insisted that the guy be at least eighteen years old. When Dan arrived, Maurice paid the pimp, who quickly disappeared, and then invited the rather young guy into his bedroom for Maurice's first sexual contact. The initiation was cold and lasted less than eleven minutes. Nothing more than mutual masturbation, but at least Maurice had touched another guy's cock for the first time.

The following week, Maurice again called Male Escort, but this time he insisted on a partner whom he could kiss and suck. "That's possible, but you have to pay twenty-five dollars more." No sooner said than done. Tim looked barely eighteen, barely let Maurice kiss him, and barely sucked him. On the other hand, Maurice could suck Tim's thick dick. Bing! Bang! Over!

But not really, in fact. A few days later, there was a knock on the door and Maurice was facing two policemen.

"Can we come in?" the older policeman asked.

Maurice asked, "What do you want?"

"To ask a few questions about your call to Male Escort."

"I requested a guy at least eighteen years old," explained Maurice.

The policeman replied, "The criminal code says homosexuality is legal between two twenty-one-year-old men, minimum."

The second policeman—younger and more polite—quickly added that they couldn't care less about what had happened behind Maurice's closed doors. They only wanted his help to arrest the pimp in charge of what was known as the homosexual vice ring.

But after Maurice described the two visits and signed a witness statement, he was arrested for gross indecency. *Oh my gosh, I went courting for the first time, and I'm going to end up in criminal court*, he thought.

When Maurice appeared in the provincial court, criminal division, his lawyer asked if the young guy across the bench was one of the escorts.

"No, I've never seen him before," answered Maurice.

Realizing that they had the wrong witness, the Crown addressed the judge: "Your Honor, we request that the trial be postponed for a week to complete the work of a very complicated case."

Maurice's lawyer sprang up immediately. "I object, Your Honor. My client has already been subjected to the media's snarling, not to mention the ostracism by his community. It is indecent to want to prosecute without the slightest evidence. This is an abuse of procedure."

The judge agreed and dismissed the case.

Maurice was relieved, though disappointed that the media did not report his acquittal. On the other hand, this experience had given him enough confidence to make a visit that would change his life. A poster on a telephone pole announced a gay drop-in every Friday night near Maurice's apartment. He told himself, *I'm not alone, I'm not a sissy, and I'm not a faggot. I'm gay, and I can meet other guys like me.*

The drop-in was hosted by Gays of Ottawa in a co-op building. The following Friday evening, Maurice timidly entered the room and was warmly welcomed by another French Canadian. Many of the attendees were civil servants in their late twenties, just like him. Maurice's coming-out started that September night in 1974.

Because the organization didn't have a liquor license, they served only soft drinks from seven to nine o'clock. Then a group would usually go for a beer at closing time, and Maurice joined them. To his surprise, they gathered in the downstairs bar of a signature hotel that was quietly known to be gay friendly. Each week, Maurice discovered a new facet of an underground culture that he had never suspected existed right there in the nation's capital—a gay counseling telephone line, a library offering gay and lesbian books, a park known for man-to-man cruising, a gay dance in a community center two or three times a year, and more.

Most of all, Maurice met a few sex partners who taught him more than mutual masturbation and sixty-nine. He'd had no idea that there were so many shades of gay.

1.6 The Gardener's Helper

The For Sale sign had been there for over a month, though many potential buyers had visited the bungalow house. Then one morning Maurice, the neighbor, was outside gardening when a family—parents and a teenaged boy—were escorted in for a visit. Two days later, a Sold sign appeared.

The house was at the end of a quiet street, away from prying eyes. Every time Maurice stepped outside to mow the lawn, prune the rosebush, or water the tomato and cucumber plants, the teenager would nonchalantly approach the fence. Maurice had noticed, during the family's initial visit, how the boy—probably seventeen or eighteen years old—had glanced at him a couple of times. Maurice read in this discreet presence a hidden interest and took advantage of the situation.

"Hi there, what's your name?" he asked.

"Edward," the boy replied coyly, "but my parents call me Teddy."

"I'm Maurice, and I need a teddy bear to help me out." Maurice smiled at Teddy.

Teddy replied, "My parents won't mind. They're gone for the weekend."

"Well, come on over. You pick the ripe tomatoes, and I'll pick the cucumbers."

The basket was full in less than ten minutes, and Maurice offered Teddy a glass of lemonade. As they sat in the backyard, far from any onlookers, Maurice didn't lose time in getting to the point.

"You look great in denim shorts," he said. "Your slim legs and firm butt stand out."

"Thank you, sir. I do a lot of bicycling."

"No, no, my name is Maurice, but you can call me Moe. You're the cutest helper I've ever had."

"I like to give a hand to people older than me. You're also very handsome, Moe."

"Nice of you to say that," replied Maurice, thinking, *I have an idea about how he can give me a hand.* He continued, "How old are you? Probably not eighteen, I suppose."

"Yes, I turned eighteen last month. I know I look younger, but I'm well developed. And you?"

Maurice wondered, *Does he want to know whether my lunch is developed or how old I am?* "Oh, I'm an old-timer. Just turned sixty."

"I'm sure you have lots of experience to share," Teddy said.

Maurice asked, "Like what? I'm just a former male nurse."

"I meant … personal. Maybe about approaching … people."

"Any schoolgirl in mind?" asked Maurice, thinking, *I doubt it.*

"No, not really interested in girls. Tried to date one or two, but they're so complicated."

Maurice asked, "No other sort of dates?"

"Not yet," Teddy answered, opening his legs and showing off a bulging crotch.

"I see," said Maurice. "It's getting hot in more ways than one, and we're both sweating. Would you like to take a shower?"

"At your place? I won't be imposing?"

"Of course not. We can shower together—to save water, to save the planet, lol."

Taking the lead, Maurice undressed and plastered a thick cock on Teddy's blond nest. The kid smiled and pulled down his jean shorts. He was wearing no underwear, and a gorgeous dick popped out so naturally that Moe embraced him while moving under the showerhead. He soaped his "helper," who reciprocated timidly at first—but with more vigor as he noticed how Moe's dick inflated.

Teddy said, "I saw my dad in the shower, but his penis looks small compared with yours."

"He probably didn't have a hard-on," Maurice replied.

"Guess not. Can I touch your cock? I've never done this before."

"It's only natural, Teddy. You can touch my pistol, caress my rod, squeeze my joystick, lick my bazooka, suck my pump."

"You're so imaginative. My English teacher would give you an A-plus in composition."

"Forget about school," Maurice said. "Let's have fun."

They both lay down on the king-size bed, and Moe began caressing Teddy's slim, soft, almost hairless body. Moaning with pleasure, the boy bragged that his tent pole had never become that tall while masturbating alone.

Before sucking the boy's trouser meat, Moe caressed his nut package. "This is a fucking nice pink grapefruit!" He tickled it with his tongue, moved upward to wrap his lips around the succulent mushroom, and chewed it slightly, triggering raving moans. The boy was ecstatic. Moe then slowly slid his tongue over the erect pink-headed soldier, so pleased that Teddy was circumcised. It didn't take much sucking to make the boy explode.

"When one is sucked for the first time, it's natural to erupt quickly," explained Maurice. "When your body has been waiting for this kind of manly pleasure, you can hardly stop the volcano's eruption."

"It never felt so good," Teddy exclaimed. "I knew you had experience to share."

"And you can feel good by sucking me, Teddy. If I take the lead, it's called face fucking."

In two steps and three measures, Moe stuffed his cock into Teddy's virgin mouth, shoving it in and out to the rhythm of a famous tune by the Village People: "It's fun to stay at the Y-M-C-A."

At the point of shooting his nectar, Moe pulled out, creamed Teddy's face, and licked it while kissing the sweet young lips. The next step was honoring the virgin ass … but that's another story, my friends.

Teddy's first gay sex experience was a dream come true. He was appreciated and felt better about his sexual orientation, thanks to Moe.

1.7 A Dream Becomes a Reality

Min Joon Sohn, alias Edward, is a Korean who moved to Halifax, Canada, for his PhD in computer science. At thirty-two, he is a closeted gay man "in principle," because he has not yet had any homosexual contact. Even though he has never touched, kissed, or dated a man, Edward fantasizes about meeting an older gentleman between forty-five and ninety. He became a member of an online gay dating service "mainly to read the profiles of various salt-and-pepper virile-looking dudes."

Paul is a seventy-one-year-old French-Canadian gay writer living in Toronto. Noticing that Edward had checked his profile, Paul decided to invite him for a chat about what it means to be gay and proud.

Edward responded immediately. "Hi, Paul. Thank you for your message. I just have vague interests here. As I mentioned in my profile, I have no experience with gay stuff. I want to know about gay people because I'm attracted to men. Joining this group and posting my profile required a lot of courage, to be honest. However, I don't want people around me to know about my sexual identity. My subscription fee does not enable me to use the chat room, but if you're okay with exchanging email messages, I'll appreciate it."

Paul thanked Edward for his trust and felt instantly at ease with the five-foot-seven Korean guy weighing 187 pounds. He could see only Edward's lips on the profile pic, but they were really sweet. Paul wrote back and explained that his profile had a heavy sexual connotation (fetish for jockstraps, rimming freak) because of the nature of Salt and Pepper Partners' website. "But don't misunderstand me. I'm a warm and affectionate guy, romantic in many ways. To show how I feel comfortable with you, Edward, I'm sending photos of myself back to age fourteen."

It took almost a week for Edward to send a full-face pic, but he was prompt in expressing his desire to meet Paul. Edward called to see if they would "click" in a direct conversation, which they did wholeheartedly. "It's only a two-hour flight from Halifax to Toronto," he told Paul. "I can be at Pearson International Airport tomorrow morning."

Paul pinched himself to be sure he wasn't dreaming.

Lo and behold, Paul and Edward met less than eight hours later. On his way to the airport, Paul wondered what he had gotten himself into, but as soon as they met at the arrivals gate, they smiled and hugged warmly. Paul shortened Edward's name and called him Ted, since that sounded friendlier, and got absolutely no opposition from the handsome Korean man.

Paul had planned to serve as tour guide and show Ted around Toronto—CN Tower, Royal Ontario Museum, Casa Loma, Toronto Islands, and even Niagara Falls.

"Fuck tourism. I want man-to-man pleasure," said Ted. Not exactly in those words, since his English was still hesitant, but his wish was loud and clear. Min Joon Sohn, alias Edward, alias Ted, was there to discover a new sex world, not attractions in a new city.

Ted had read that Paul was excited to see guys in tight blue jeans, so that's what he was wearing, knowing it could trigger a spanking. The slap kind of hurt, especially near the balls, but Paul explained that pain can sometimes be pleasurable. Still, he limited his hand swing to the thighs and wide butt of his new playmate.

Ted embraced Paul warmly and kissed him tenderly. Then his French-Canadian coach gave him a lesson in French kissing, and Ted was eager to reciprocate— and also to suck something else. In two steps and three movements, the new couple was in the sixty-nine position, and they both had small but loaded pistols. Ted's balls were nice to squeeze, lick, swallow, and even chew.

Paul called their cock-to-cock frotting a "cocktail," and he loved pushing the tip of his tongue into Ted's pee hole. *I'm rimming his dick, and it's fucking nice!*

Maybe because of stress or nerves, they didn't reach explosion, but that had no effect on their pleasure. The warm and tender feelings were more important than a physical outburst.

The distance between the balls and the anus—perineum—was a golden path for Paul. He enjoyed burying his face in the virile crack, smelling the manly aroma, licking the doughnut, sucking the rosebud, and tongue twisting his way inside the satanic haven. Ted moaned at each step, which encouraged Paul to be more aggressive. "Your ass is divine, Ted," he exclaimed. "You are my teddy bear! I want to grab your buns and tickle them with my beard."

Rimming was something Ted had barely read about, but he quickly discovered that his star-shaped anus excited Paul, and he had a lot of fun offering his smooth Asian ass. Ashamed of his too-wide butt a few days earlier, Ted was now handsomely proud of his generous behind—or *derrière*, as Paul liked to call it.

Fucking was not at the top of Paul and Ted's priorities. Oral fun ranked first, and they engaged in kissing, licking, sucking, and rimming before breakfast, lunch, dinner, and night sleep. The only sad part of their encounter was walking back to Union Station so that Ted could catch the express train for the airport. Was it "See you later," "Goodbye," or "Farewell"? Time would tell.

2

Interracial

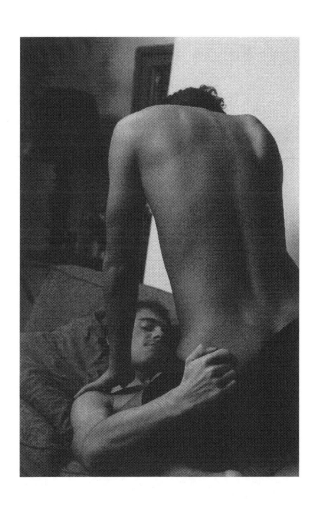

2.1 Bronze Monument to Virility

T hat afternoon, the gym wasn't too busy. By the time Paul had done a little more than half of his workout, he and a black guy were the only remaining clients. Paul had a hard time concentrating on the weight exercises because he constantly had a firm butt at his reach. And the owner of that butt kept scratching his crotch. Was that a message?

The stars seemed well aligned, because the two guys headed for the shower at the same time. Paul followed the bronze guy, who seemed to be forty-five to fifty years old. He discreetly watched him remove his gym shorts and was amazed by the scene: a perfect incarnation of the two hemispheres.

When Paul approached him in the shower, the dude stepped backward and said, "I'm for rent. Cash only."

"No problem. Is a dollar a minute okay?" asked Paul.

"No, I won't take less than two dollars a minute."

"Hired. I'm Paul. What's your name?"

"Michael, but my intimate friends call me Adonis."

"I can see why, Adonis. You're mouthwatering."

He was a mature Adonis with the butt of a young stallion. Paul relished the scenario he was imagining for his hired dude.

When they reached his apartment, Paul indicated that since he was paying, he was giving the orders. And since Adonis was wearing tight faded jeans, the first order was "On your knees. You're in for a spanking." Rather than slapping Adonis's butt, Paul directed his hand inside the crotch where the jean seams met. That triggered a slight "Ouch!" at first, followed by moans of pleasure.

Adonis was six foot one and weighed about 220 pounds, but there wasn't one ounce of fat on his athletic body. Paul ordered his rent man to remove everything except his jockstrap and then stand at attention. In front of him stood a bronze monument to virility.

"I'm going to lick, kiss, bite and suck every inch of your fucking body," Paul said.

"Sorry, but I'm not keen on kissing a stranger on the lips."

"Will an extra dollar a minute change your disposition?"

"Yes, sir!" exclaimed Adonis.

"That's the way I like it. You call me sir from now on."

Paul choreographed an oral ballet in which Adonis proved a bit hesitant at first, but gradually he became a pure slut. Paul didn't have to give the next order, for Adonis positioned himself for a sixty-nine exam, and then master and slave sucked each other's hard dicks with appetite. Cut or uncut, the rod always offers a succulent mushroom.

Feeling that Adonis was almost on the verge of cumming or making soup, Paul abruptly stopped and said, "Don't cum now. The best is yet to come."

"What do you mean, sir?" asked Adonis.

"I want to rim you."

"My partner isn't into that, but I adore it."

"You're in for a treat," said Paul, "but I'll deduct a dollar for that period since I'm the one who's giving the pleasure."

"You're a nasty negotiator, sir, and I'm your obedient servant."

Paul slid his tongue onto Adonis's cock, balls, and ass crack to reach the anus. "In French, we call it *rosette* or rosebud." Sir darted his servant's asshole with fervor—spitting on it, licking and kissing it voraciously, savoring the aroma of masculinity. Adonis was ready to explode, but Paul said, "Wait, I want to drink your nectar!" Back in the sixty-nine position, they engaged in the last steps of the choreography to swallow a creamy load.

Then Adonis, who was an accountant, looked at his watch and made a rough calculation. "You're at about two hundred dollars. To be honest, I'm not a rent man. I just said that because you looked so interested and you could be my father, age-wise. But if I like older guys, and if I can visit once a week, there's no charge."

Paul and Adonis shook hands and kissed greedily.

When Adonis left the apartment, Paul gave a firm slap to the delicious ass tightly wrapped in faded blue jeans. "Next week, you get to wear my red jockstrap."

"Can hardly wait, sir!"

2.2 North Meets South

Jean-Paul was raised in a French-Canadian family where the French language was placed on a pedestal. For high school, his parents sent him to a Catholic boarding school some five hundred miles away in the nation's capital, Ottawa. The only boy in a family of four kids, Jean-Paul—known to his friends as JP—was glad to evolve in a male environment and participate in sports such as volleyball and hockey.

At bedtime, the resident boys had to undress modestly in front of their lockers, hiding in their bathrobes. But JP could not resist glancing at his friend Robin, who liked to show off his penis. One night JP followed Robin into the shower room, and the boys entered side-by-side booths. The prefect of discipline ensured that shower doors were closed, but JP was tall enough to see over the separating wall and admire the athletic Robin under the water jet.

November 1 was All Saints Day, and the boarding school residents could go home for a day or two. Since JP lived too far away, Robin invited him home for the holiday. That night, when they were ready to go to sleep, JP realized that he and Robin would have to share a bed.

"No need to wear pajamas," Robin said. "The blanket will keep you warm."

JP replied, "You know, I've never slept just in underwear. I'm a little chilly."

"Don't worry, I'll warm you up as best as I can. By the way, I sleep naked," Robin said.

"I saw you completely naked in the shower."

"Yes, I know, and I think you liked it, hey?"

"Uh … Yes, maybe," admitted JP.

On this timid admission of interest, Robin slapped JP's butt and cuddled against him.

It didn't take JP long to notice that Robin's penis was different. JP never used words like *cock*, *dick*, or *rod*, preferring the French word *bizoune*, which had an exotic—and erotic—note. "Can I touch it?" he asked his friend.

Robin answered, "Yes, but you have to remove your slip."

Unlike Robin, JP was circumcised, which led to meticulous examination on both sides. Handling each other's cocks triggered a pair of erections, and Robin began jerking his friend's dick.

"Isn't this a sin … a mortal sin?" JP asked.

"No way, since we're not hurting anyone."

"You're right, Robin. It feels so good."

Robin encouraged his friend, "Put more energy into it, JP!"

In less than two minutes, the two boys exploded with pleasure. Robin had to put his hand on JP's mouth to prevent him from voicing his joy too loudly and thus alerting the parents downstairs.

Thanks to this experience, JP realized that he was more attracted to boys than girls. At the university, he frequently cruised a classmate nerd, succeeding once or twice in engaging in mutual masturbation behind a campus building, and a fellow philosophy student taught him about fellatio. Sucking was succulent, but being sucked was divine!

The year he graduated, JP was chosen to represent young French Canadians at the International Francophone Youth Summit, held for the first time in Yamoussoukro, the capital of Ivory Coast. In addition to workshops, roundtables, and conferences on how to promote the preservation of French, the summit offered a few excursion tours. JP chose a guided visit to a sugarcane plantation in Zuenoula.

The guide was a thirty-four-year-old man, the most handsome black guy JP had ever seen. Slender with short frizzy hair, luscious lips, muscled biceps, and round buttocks, Marcel was endowed with all the attributes needed to seduce JP, who had been noticing the discreet winks thrown at him by the guide.

There was free time after the tour, so JP approached Marcel and said, "I really liked your presentation."

"Thank you," said Marcel. "I can show you more if you want."

"Like what, for example?"

Marcel said, "Follow me into the warehouse."

When the door was closed and locked, Marcel delicately caressed JP's face and kissed his mouth. The intoxication was instantaneous. For both men, it was their first interracial encounter. In no time, they were completely naked.

JP was amazed to see how well-endowed Marcel was. His erect bizoune was eight inches long. *Wow!* A magnificent pink acorn emerged from a splendid black tail and stimulated JP, so eager to suck it dry.

Marcel had chosen the warehouse because there was a sleeping bag in the corner for the night-shift security guard. He directed JP to the thin mattress, and then he made his dream come true—black and white harmony in a sixty-nine swing. JP had often been told that he had a big mouth, and now was his chance to validate that observation. Marcel, on the other hand, had the opportunity to do wonders with his luscious lips and even indulge in his partner's full lunch—tail and balls.

Soon both were moaning with pleasure, a prelude to a volcanic eruption. JP had never known that Ivorian nectar could be so creamy, and Marcel learned how succulent Canadian cum could be.

That day, JP knew that he would return to Ivory Coast, the cornucopia.

2.3 East Meets West

On a warm summer afternoon, an athletic Neemun invited his close artistic friend Georges to exercise with him on the bicycle path of Toronto's Centre Island in Lake Ontario. At sixty-six, Georges was a French-Canadian book critic at least twice the age of Neemun, a Chinese hairdresser, but this was not a barrier for dynamic get-togethers. Both dudes liked bicycling, picnicking, visiting the Art Gallery of Ontario, going to concerts, or just reading at home while tasting a glass of Niagara wine and Canadian cheddar cheese.

The bicycling expedition was always an opportunity to admire Toronto's burgeoning landscape around the majestic CN Tower, completed in 1976 and rising 1,815 feet. CN had held the record for the world's tallest freestanding structure for thirty-two years, but Neemun never missed the opportunity to remind Georges that the Shanghai Tower in his home city was at least 250 feet taller.

"Okay, my dear," Georges would concede, "but the

CN Tower remains the tallest freestanding structure in the Western Hemisphere." The discussion always ended with a kiss, the best way for East and West to meet.

This traditional summer expedition also helped the two friends build an appetite, so Georges would always offer to prepare a cold plate in his condo on the waterfront. Neemun would ask him to put on some music—maybe a Village People album, since Georges had always imagined Neemun as "Macho Man." As for the cold plate, it included slices of tomato and cucumber, asparagus tips wrapped in Black Forest ham, and avocados stuffed with crabmeat and artichoke hearts, accompanied by pumpernickel bread and foie gras, each ingredient having been carefully selected at the St. Lawrence Market. Georges had a hard time preparing the meal because Neemun was always brushing against him in the kitchen, blowing a kiss on his cheeks or pinching his ass.

When they sat down for dinner, the sun had set and the romantic Neemun had lit candles, which accentuated his energizing brown eyes. Georges's smile was highlighted by his white beard, which had been shortly trimmed. He suggested starting with an asparagus tip for two, an old trick in which they started at opposite ends of a tip, met in the middle, and topped it with a kiss. Again, East and West met succulently.

After the meal, Neemun and Georges always cuddled on the love seat. Even if there was a book to read and review, Georges knew that some cute distraction would prevent him from turning more than three or four pages. They would engage in an exchange of love words in Chinese and French. Neemun would first whisper, "*Gaofushuai*" (tall, rich, and cute), to which Georges would reply, "*Mon pitou*" (my puppy). Then "*Da bao*" (big treasure) would trigger "*Ma chouette*" (my little owl). Inevitably Neemun's hand would slowly caress Georges's thighs, exercising more and more pressure as it reached a bulging crotch.

Then it would be time to let nature follow its course, to let emotions express themselves freely. No better place to do so than on the queen-size bed. On one wall Georges had enlarged a picture of two cowboys in tight jeans and leather chaps, and three bodybuilders in jockstraps occupied the wall facing the bed—the right atmosphere for a ritual of caressing hands and kissing lips. In this preamble to a heated close encounter, Georges's favorite move was to grab Neemun's ass in tight jeans and first slap his buns, then the bottom of his crack highlighted by the sewn denim seam. That always triggered an exciting feeling of pain.

This was followed by a sensuous undressing ballet in which Georges would lick Neemun's red jockstrap, making his virility expand voluptuously. Each step was accompanied by moans of pleasure. Naked, the two partners would embrace and kiss passionately before flipping into a sixty-nine position. Georges would avidly suck the Shanghai Tower, and Neemun would swallow the entire CN Tower, as East and West again met lustfully. Georges would lose no time in gradually moving his lips into Neemun's ass crack, reaching the jackpot prize, a succulent rosette. Rimming was always at the top of Georges's libido menu.

While taking pleasure in getting his asshole licked, kissed, sucked, and tongue-twisted, Neemun would gradually switch to his preferred choreography, lubing his partner's ass, fingering it aggressively, covering his cock with whipped cream, slowly entering Georges's dark corner, pounding him until he exploded, and then mixing cream and cum to improvise a unique sundae. "What a dessert, my da bao!" he would exclaim.

After this wild choreography, the two dudes would embrace and kiss romantically. Neemun would then use Georges's belly as a pillow, slowly fall asleep, and slide into a lascivious dream.

2.4 Cult of the Bronze Butt

É tienne, a sixty-eight-year-old Canadian, has been corresponding with Didier, a thirty-six-year-old guy from Togo, on the south coast of West Africa. They met online thanks to the Silver Daddies dating site. Étienne and Didier are very different: white and black, sixty-eight and thirty-six, chubby and slim, out and closeted, professional and blue collar, and six-inch cock and nine-inch cock (though both are circumcised). Étienne likes younger guys and Didier is attracted to older men, so they're a perfect match despite the geographical distance.

As soon as they met online, the two men exchanged email addresses and many pictures. Étienne first sent photos taken when he was fourteen, twenty-six, thirty-one, and sixty-two, all with glasses. In the last photo, he's bald and wearing a red jockstrap. Didier first shared a serious face pic highlighting his gorgeous thick lips, followed by two strange illustrations probably found on the internet. The first was a 2019 New Year's greeting card with a naked slim black guy in a push-up position, his long, erect cock serving as the digit *1* in *2019*. The second pic was a white dick locked in a chastity belt, representing Didier's difficulty engaging in man-to-man pleasure with a white man.

In each reply to Étienne's messages, Didier added a new photo—one of his hairless six-pack, a close-up in a tight black-and-white-striped brief, another in a bulging pink-and-blue undie. He asked his new friend to send personal photos, but without a smartphone, old-fashioned Étienne had no way to send selfies. He did forward a few official photos taken when he had received the Order of Canada, a medal from the Canadian Senate and the Queen's Jubilee medal, and Diddier was quite impressed.

Even though he could not send erotic pics of himself, Étienne insisted on receiving a selfie of Didier in the shower with a hard-on. He was more than pleased when his African friend sent a pic of his soft dick and another of his full-blown erect rod above a saucer of thick white cum. To be fair, Étienne asked a close friend to take a picture of his small penis and flat ass, which he included in his next email, along with a request now for a photo of Didier's butt.

No sooner said than done. Étienne felt like he was in the National Gallery admiring Rodin's *The Age of Bronze* (*L'Âge d'airain*). This bronze life-size statue by the French sculptor Auguste Rodin is a figure of a nude male, seventy-two inches high. Rodin had the Belgian soldier

Auguste Ney pose for the statue. It is partly inspired by Michelangelo's *Dying Slave* in the Louvre, which has the elbow raised above the head. If Didier had posed for Rodin, *The Age of Bronze* would obviously show off a much bigger cock.

Rodin presented his statue for the first time at the 1877 Salon de Paris. The reaction surprised him because some critics went as far as accusing Rodin of having casted a living model. He denied this accusation vigorously, but he benefited from the false insinuation since a large public was eager to admire the "critical" statue. Casts of the sculpture can now be found in many museums around the world: Paris, London, Rome, Berlin, Dublin, Tokyo, Budapest, Glasgow, Mexico City, Lisbon, Barcelona, Canada's National Gallery, and many US cities, such as San Francisco, Philadelphia, Washington, DC, and Dallas.

For Étienne, *The Age of Bronze*'s butt remained a perfect illustration of the sensuous curve of Didier's bronze asset: round, firm, nicely parted like two small hemispheres, a direct invitation for a caress, a kiss, a slurp, a bite, a tongue attack, a dick slap in the crack, and, of course, a powerful thrust that Étienne could only lustfully imagine. He decided to enlarge a picture of Didier's frontal selfie in the shower and of Rodin's male nude seen from the back, which he plastered on either side of his queen-size bed—a romantic way of sleeping with a long-distance friend.

Was it a cliché, or were black butts more appetizing than white, yellow, and red rear ends? Étienne thought they were definitely rounder and more prominent, thus attracting more attention. Since he was a rimming king, he dreamed of sucking Didier's dark rosebud while paying homage to Rodin's bronze *chef-d'œuvre*. When he first saw the reproduction in the National Gallery of Canada, in Ottawa, he could not resist caressing the butt. He had to wait until the coast was clear—no visitors, no security guard, just a chance to kiss it tenderly and quickly whisper a little poem:

O ass of ebony
Divine offering
On the altar of virility
You make me hard
O plump loaf
In the temple of Black Beauty
I knead you frantically
You make me drool with pleasure
O living and enticing map
Of the two hemispheres
I sail in your furrow
To deposit my foam
O appetizing roundness
That I'm avidly biting
Before giving you a spank
That stirs up your libido

O intoxicating hindquarters
You're getting my dick drunk
You invite it to enter
Your satanic lair

2.5 The Poetry of Long-Distance Love

Paul and Marcel are in love, but they have never met face-to-face. Paul is seventy-one and lives in Canada; Marcel is thirty-five and lives in Ivory Coast. The Silver Daddies website brought them together. They first communicated through the message box of the site, exchanging email addresses, and it wasn't long before "daddy and son" were sending each other photos and affectionate letters.

The age and race differences play a major role in this relationship. Marcel is black, slim, and young with a firm round butt, well endowed, cut, and cute—everything Paul likes in a virile partner. Paul is a nice-looking senior, bald with a beard, a hairy belly, and a small cut dick—exactly what Marcel seeks in a potential husband.

When making contact with an interesting party on the Silver Daddies site, Paul gets the ball rolling by sending a series of photos from age fourteen to the present. This usually triggers a warm reception and leads the two parties to talk about their brothers and sisters, their work experience, their hobbies, their favorite music, and most of all, their sexual preferences, fantasies, and fetishes.

Paul has a heavy fetish for guys in jockstraps or leather gear, and he finds pictures of black men in that attire to show how he imagines Marcel on a first sexual encounter. These visuals add some spice to his emails. As for the young Ivorian, he dreams of a white-haired man sucking his thick long shaft, and the internet provides him with a good gallery of photos. Marcel even found a picture of a white cock locked in a chastity belt, a symbol of what he cannot easily get. Homosexuality is not illegal in Ivory Coast, but being gay can be dangerous because homophobes will beat up gay men, so Marcel is in the closet.

As a writer and book critic, Paul doesn't lose time in sending a short poem inspired by an Ellie Goulding song:

How long will I love my dear Marcel?
As long as the stars are above our heads.
How long will I hold my sweet Marcel?
As long as the virile perfume engulfs us.
How long will I give to my blessed Marcel?
As long as the fusion energizes us.

Just as poetic words touch the soul, erotic pictures touch the body—and we all know that a picture is worth a thousand words. Paul invites Marcel to take selfies in the shower. "I want to see your bronze butt, your divine offering!" He not only sees a cute little behind, but also a huge cock, a stiff ramrod, even a dripping weapon over his mouth. *So fucking tasty!*

Daddy does not have a smartphone and cannot send selfies to Marcel. On the other hand, he has published two poetry books in French—*Homoportrait* and *Homosecret*—that he sends to his son via Canada Post. Mail delivery in Ivory Coast is not like in Canada; it can take weeks. Paul learns that for two dollars more on his monthly Bell Canada telephone bill, he can call around the world as often as he wants. *Great! I can read erotic poems to my sweetheart and hear him moan with appreciation, with man-to-man pleasure.*

> If I like them frail and timid,
> It is to better dominate them.
> If I prefer them wounded or fragile,
> It is to better possess them.
> If I wish them frisky and brawling,
> It is to better tame them.
> If I want them complicit or expansive,
> It is to better penetrate them.

Paul is obviously a top in bed, while Marcel is a bottom who likes to crunch a French fry, sip an aperitif, drink from the neck, stretch the macaroni, or swallow the whiting. With the sausage or the blood pudding, it becomes serious, and the mushroom grows at full speed.

To describe the virile member, Alfred de Musset spoke of a rudder; today it looks more like paraphernalia. Ronsard gave it the name of *flambante chandelle* (flaming candle), which is no doubt why we are so eager to put a torch in the repository, so to speak. Zola called it the human beast for whom it is always noon to its clock.

Paul calls around 6:00 p.m., 10:00 p.m. Ivory Coast time, to tuck Marcel into bed and sing him a poetic lullaby.

A daddy in Canada, a son in Ivory Coast, and words and photos that unite them. Will such a love relationship last, let alone materialize? Time will tell, because this is a true story.

2.6   Mouthwatering Delicacies

aka is a thirty-five-year-old Japanese guy, five foot nine, 143 pounds. He defines himself as bottom and oral versatile. When you see a picture of Taka at age seventeen or eighteen, you imagine that he could have inspired the artist Ben Kimura, the face of Japanese gay magazines such as *Barazoku* and *Sabu*.

All Kimura drawings portray idealized yet alluringly masculine bodies. The faces are boyish with realistic expressions: petulant, moody, brooding, soulful, or pouty, yet always sensuous. Like Kimura's boys, Taka is completely hairless, except maybe for a little black tuft down there. He trains in the gym at least four times a week and likes to wear a white jockstrap, which he proudly exhibits in the locker room. His charm attracts guys his own age and elderly men salivating with concupiscence.

In the shower, Taka is often approached by slim young gymnasts who show off their thick dicks and offer to rub his back, not to mention his back door. Taka always turns around quickly in the hope of finding someone equally straightforward but twice his age. Ever since he discovered his sexual orientation, the attraction of a father figure has been predominant.

Is it because he was raised by a single mother? Is it because he seeks to be dominated by an iron fist in a velvet glove? Is it because he's looking for the experience of a man at the height of maturity? One thing is certain: Taka wants to serve as a sex toy for a dream daddy, uncle, godfather, or senior gentleman. And since he moved to New York, that male figure must be white—a rice queen in the gay community.

On Sunday afternoons, Taka takes a stroll in Central Park. He often notices a white man, roughly sixty-five, reading on a bench and discreetly smiling as Taka walks by. He who risks nothing gets nothing, so Taka makes the first move.

"Hello. What are you reading?" he asks the man.

"Confessions of a Mask by Kuki Mishima," the man answers

"He's one of my compatriots," says Taka, "and he's my favorite Japanese author."

"I wondered if you were Chinese, Japanese, or Korean. My name's Paul."

"My name is Taka. I'm from Osaka and moved to New York six years ago."

Paul says, "Please sit down. Maybe we can discuss Mishima's struggle to fit into Japanese society."

Taka explains to Paul that Kochan, the name of the

protagonist in *Confessions of a Mask*, is the diminutive of the author's real name, Kimitake. Like Mishima, Kochan was born with a less-than-ideal body in terms of physical fitness and robustness.

Paul comments that throughout the first half of the book, Kochan struggles intensely to fit into Japanese society. He is portrayed as a weak homosexual who is kept away from boys his own age, some of whom might have the same inclination.

"This isolation leads Kochan to his future fascination and fantasies about same-sex experiences," says Taka.

"In that sense, isn't Mishima similar to Kochan?" asks Paul. "Is it not an autobiographical novel?"

Taka says, "Indeed, and similar to my own experience, although mine was much more modest."

"I kind of guessed that you're gay. So am I, and I'm pleased to meet you, Taka."

"Same here, Paul. I feel comfortable with you. Would you be free for dinner tonight?"

Paul replies, "I never say no to a golden opportunity to admire masculinity."

"Like me, you probably enjoyed looking at Roman sculptures of men in dynamic physical poses when you were young," says Taka.

On that promising note, Paul suggests that they pick up fresh shrimp, sushi, and a bottle of wine and enjoy a meal in his studio condo overlooking the Hudson River.

His plan is already laid out in black and white—or white and yellow, in this case.

Taka is glad that he's wearing a jockstrap and tight faded blue jeans. It makes him feel horny and ready to attack the pièce de résistance.

Finger food and a glass of wine go hand in hand when the two men are cuddling on the sofa. Paul proposes that the entire evening be enjoyed under the theme "mouthwatering delicacies." For Taka, that means kissing, sucking, and rimming—exactly what's at the top of his sensuous menu. Paul's queen-size bed becomes an arena for naked combat. The two men wrestle to kiss each other's lips, dicks, balls, asses. Taka keeps saying, "Use me as a sex toy. I have the feeling that I'm hugging the warmest teddy bear I've ever met."

The pièce de résistance is the hidden jewel, the rosebud, the smelly freckle, the butthole. In attacking it, licking it, sucking it, and tongue darting it, Paul and Taka feel in perfect harmony. As Elton John's song goes, they're pretty good company, and they want to let their feelings flow and love each other forever.

3

Daddies

3.1 Fuck, They Are All So Damn Hot!

We hear that a picture is worth a thousand words, but Julien disagrees. He would even say that most pictures on the daddy-son dating site are worth only one word: *fuck!* Many guys choose to show either their huge erect cock or their savvy butthole. They want to fuck or be fucked. Julien is versatile, and he appreciates the front and back doors, so to speak. His profile on the dating site, however, is accompanied by a face pic and a head-to-toe photo—not in the nude, but in a jockstrap to indicate his fetish.

Julien's online cruising name is Gay1976, the year that he came out. Here's his profile info:

Age: seventy-one

Height: six foot two

Weight: 202 pounds

City: Toronto

Country: Canada

Sexually is: oral versatile

Seeking: a date, friend, sex partner, relationship

Prefer men aged: thirty-five to fifty-five

Unlike many older men, Julien's profile text is not limited to something like "looking for younger hot dudes to have fun with." He invites potential partners to read a detailed road map spelled out in five paragraphs:

"Affectionate, romantic, and bilingual (French-English), I'm looking for a man with whom I can talk, cuddle, hug, and kiss before heading to the bedroom. I'm a writer and book critic, and I've published gay novels and short stories, plus essays on homosexuality and the French-speaking community of Ontario.

"A leader in bed, I like to caress your crotch in a jockstrap (will lend you one), massage your tight buns, frottage before stripping naked, then suck slowly and firmly, enjoy 69, gradually lick and chew your balls (if you want), and slide my tongue into your ass to rim you with frenzy. Can gladly slap your ass if desired. I like the smell of virility—a clean but sweaty ass is the best perfume!

"I don't need to cum. Foreplay suits me well. Being top for me consists of fingering your firm ass and biting it, if you like that. White, black, or Asian asses drive me crazy! No anal penetration, active or passive.

"You are a little submissive, you like dirty talk, you are cut or uncut (I'm cut), you can wear tight jeans (more exciting if you enjoy slapping), the best you can offer me is your rosebud to rim. The only drug I take is insulin to control my diabetes."

The online dating site is renowned internationally,

and Julien immediately receives messages from countries a world apart: Russia and the United States. The Russian guys are usually in their midtwenties and fall in love after two or three emails. Julien cautions them, "I'm just a friendly pen pal," but the love letters keep pouring in. He tries to put an end to these exchanges by asking his Russian correspondents to send him a photo of their hard dicks, their firm butts, their mouthwatering assholes—he now has a collection of pics that would have made the American pornographic monthly magazine *Playguy* jealous.

Stanislav, a young Russian correspondent from St. Petersburg, is an artist and promises to draw a picture of his "Canadian daddy." A week later, he tells Julien that he was robbed when getting on the bus, and all his arts supplies were in the packsack that was taken. Softhearted Julien sends him a hundred dollars via Western Union. A week later, Stanislav writes a long letter to say that he is in a hospital on death row unless he gets an operation that can cost up to six thousand dollars. "My mother has put up our house for sale, but we need the money now. Please help me! I promise to reimburse more than this amount." Julien's answer is quick and blunt: "I don't believe one word of your phony letter. Get lost!"

On the American side, Julien exchanges with a Californian cowboy correspondent. His huge bulging crotch in tight blue jeans is highlighted by leather chaps and boots, a dress code that makes Julien salivate. Soon that photo is serving as a background on his computer screen, often triggering a jerk-off session. *Fuck, this Joey is so damn hot, I would love to suck him off dry!* But after barely a week of correspondence, Joey's true nature spills out: "I need your help, just $1,000. Can you be my sugar daddy?" Julien can't believe that Joey wants to suck his leather wallet dry. He immediately puts an end to that so-called friendly Canada-USA relationship.

Replies from guys in Toronto are not as frequent as from abroad. The dudes whom Julien manages to attract are immigrants from Iran, China, Korea, and Guyana. "Fuck, they are all so damn hot!" These guys really enjoy being sucked and rimmed, but when they find out that ass fucking is not on the agenda, the relationship abruptly ends. Julien has no other choice than to apply the famous verse of the sixteenth-century French poet François de Malherbe to his ephemeral situation: "And Rose, she lived as live the roses, for the space of a morning."

3.2 The Art of Tongue Dancing

t was mid-April, the sun was shining, and the cherry trees were blossoming. Easter was late that year, and the park had already attracted a small crowd. A fifty-nine-year-old man was sitting on a bench reading a hardcover book. The twenty-three-year-old guy facing him on an opposite bench seemed absorbed in some kind of textbook, but he kept glancing at the older man. When the younger one smiled, the older one detected interest and approached the handsome young man.

"I took your smile as an invitation. My name is Paul."

"You read clearly between the lines. My name is Mathew."

Paul asked, "Are you reading a university textbook?"

"Yes, I'm a law student. And you, a novel or an essay?" asked Mathew.

"A French novel," Paul replied. "I'm a book critic and author."

"Wow! What do you write?"

"Mainly essays on French-Canadian culture, but also some gay novels and homoerotic short stories."

Mathew asked, "Are they all in French? I would love to read gay romantic stories."

"Birds of the same feather flock together. Am I right, Mathew?"

"Yes, Paul, we're on the same wavelength."

In the week leading to Easter Sunday, Mathew and Paul met regularly on the park bench, sitting closer to each other each time. Mathew's smile was so energizing that Paul was tempted to embrace his new friend, who seemed to be openly gay.

Mathew said, "At a young age, I knew I was attracted to guys … older than me."

"Interesting, Mathew! I was over twenty-five when I discovered my attraction for men, and now I love the company of guys at least twenty-five or even thirty-five years younger than me."

"I guess I fall into that category. Would you like to be my special friend?" asked Mathew.

Paul said, "Yes, we could certainly learn from each other."

On Easter Sunday, Paul invited Mathew for dinner at his place. He poured a glass of sparkling wine and proposed a toast to "a blossoming friendship!" Then he served a cold plate composed of avocado stuffed with crab meat, asparagus tips wrapped in prosciutto ham, sliced tomatoes and cucumber, and carrot and orange pepper sticks, followed by a selection of Brie and Jarlsberg cheeses. Throughout the meal, Mathew kept gently brushing his knee against Paul's thigh. The dessert—or climax—was a warm embrace and light kiss on the lips.

As he and Paul cuddled on the love seat, Mathew thought how kissing was his Superman's kryptonite, but he wasn't flipping through the pages of his favorite comic book anymore. He was holding a real Superman, a hero in flesh and blood. It was time to explain what he had in mind when he had asked Paul to be his "special friend."

"Paul, can I call you Daddy?"

"Do you dream of being my son?" Paul asked.

Mathew said, "Yes, I fantasize about a daddy-son relationship."

"In what sense?"

"Well, I can learn from a mature man. For me, you're a real library."

"As a writer," said Paul, "I take that as a real compliment."

"So will you be my daddy?" Mathew asked.

"With pleasure, my son."

Every week, Paul invited Mathew for a meal, and they always had dessert on the love seat. When his new son started to rub crotch to crotch, Daddy felt aroused but couldn't react as vigorously as he wanted. He whispered to himself, "Honesty is the best policy!" Then he explained to Mathew that he'd had diabetes since the age of thirty-four and erectile problems since he was fifty-five.

"I don't easily get a hard-on, son," Paul explained.

"Don't worry, Daddy. I feel comfortable with you."

"Yes, but I can't fuck you."

Mathew asked, "Would you like to suck me?"

"Of course, but I'd like even more to rim your sweet ass."

"*Wow!*" exclaimed Mathew. "That's what I like the most. We're meant to be together."

Feeling like a load had been taken off his shoulders, Paul directed Mathew to his bedroom. Pictures of guys in jockstraps or tight jeans and leather chaps covered the wall facing the bed. When Daddy took a red jockstrap out of the dirty clothes hamper, his son smiled, grabbed it, and started to sniff it lustfully—another sign that they were meant to be together. From then on, the dress code for meals was different colored jockstraps for Daddy and son.

Paul explained to Mathew that the jockstrap was originally intended to cup and support men's genitals during sports activities such as football, hockey, and cycling. "The jockstrap is practical, functional, and comfortable, but it also has a strong sexual association because it leaves your sweet ass not only exposed but prominently on display. And I really like that!"

Mathew agreed wholeheartedly, just as Paul gently slapped his firm butt.

Daddy went on to explain that the two elastic straps were affixed not only to the base of the pouch, but also almost at the entrance of the asshole—a real turn-on for guys who like to rim their partner.

"A tongue inside my anus drives me wild, Daddy!" exclaimed Mathew.

"Unlike the head of your penis, your anus rarely gets sore or oversensitized from use. I've met some men who were so relaxed that I could work my entire tongue all the way inside, driving the quietest of them to yell out, 'Oh God! Oh fuck!'"

"Yes, your tongue is a powerful tool, Daddy. Don't stop your demonstration!"

Since his new son wanted so much to learn from a mature man, Daddy decided to show how he had been placed on earth to make men moan from pleasure. He called his "full-tongue-length inside swirl" the ultimate in rimming. Mathew learned quickly and reciprocated with verve.

Paul was now ready for the "triple whammy." He pulled his partner's balls down near the anus and licked from the asshole to the testicles and back a few times. Then he pulled Mathew's cock down and licked from the anus up to the balls, and over and around the head of the dick, and back down again to the rosebud.

"I'm all yours, Daddy. You can lick, suck, bite, and chew my offering. Let's call it tongue dancing."

"Great idea, son. We can share both words and pleasure."

3.3 Warm Welcome in Iran

J eff's last trip to Europe was a two-week tour of Turkey. At the end of the expedition, the guide offered an extension to Syria, Iran, or Georgia. Jeff chose Iran and could not have made a better selection. When he checked into his Iranian hotel, he was welcomed at the reception desk by a clerk with a name tag reading "Nima." The thirty-year-old Iranian man was so good-looking that Jeff didn't hesitate to offer a coded smile.

Nima confirmed the reservation, gave Jeff a key, and welcomed him to the Espinas Persian Gulf Hotel. Then the clerk whispered what he had practiced in English for a long time: "I finish my shift in two hours, but will knock on your door to ensure that you are comfortably installed, sir."

Jeff took a little nap after unpacking. He kept thinking of Nima's smile, manly deodorant, and virile look. Exactly two hours later, he heard a gentle knock on the door. Nima walked in carrying a tray with a large bottle of nonalcoholic beer, two glasses, a bowl of yogurt and cucumber slices, and fresh fruits. Jeff was more intrigued by the hotel clerk's attitude than by the appetizing platter.

Nima kept going around the room to make it look tidy, and every time he approached Jeff, he nonchalantly caressed his thigh or even his ass.

Jeff was twice Nima's age, but he got the message. "No need to tidy up. Why don't you sit down with me and share the beer and yogurt dip?"

"Nice of you to invite me. I can pour you a glass of Shams, sir."

"Please call me Jeff, my handsome Nima!"

The young Iranian and older Canadian cuddled on the sofa, sipped their beer, and slowly moved into a passionate embrace. Nima showered Jeff with long tender kisses that led to caresses on the cheeks, pectorals, thighs, butt, and bulging crotch. Jeff guided Nima to the king-size bed, slowly undressing him to admire the splendor of a full-blown tower of virile beauty, polishing it with his tongue. For Nima, each lick became a breath of love. Each caress went beyond the erotic body to reach the inner soul, the heart.

Nima could not believe that his dream was finally coming true. Having had little experience, he followed Jeff's lead, licking and sucking his partner's cock, chewing on his balls. When Jeff directed his tongue into Nima's asshole, there was a sudden hesitation. This was new territory for the young Iranian, but he was more than willing to learn from his new master. Nima licked timidly at first, then started to twist his tongue in Jeff's rosebud. Moans of pleasure and a hardening cock pushed Nima to jerk his partner off and trigger an explosion of nectar.

It was now Nima's turn to reach an orgasm, so Jeff used his sperm to lubricate his ass and invited his young friend to fuck him gently but firmly until full satisfaction. Nima was so excited that he wept with joy on Jeff's crack, embraced him from behind, and slapped his thick dark rod on Jeff's pale butt. Once his engine had reached full acceleration, he headed toward Jeff's one-way street of pleasure. No stop signs, just "yield to heavy traffic." Nima's hips and Jeff's buns were now bumper to bumper. The collision resulted in a load of cream.

After a quick shower, the young Iranian and older Canadian again cuddled on the sofa. Nima reminded Jeff that homosexuality is illegal in Iran, and that it's dangerous to be gay in that country. With a tear in his eye, Nima gently kissed Jeff on the lips. The time had come for him to open his heart and deliver a poem that he had prepared for the right man at the right moment:

> Oh, my dear, you look like a dove
> Like an angel sent from above
> Stay in my arms
> Let me embrace you
> Now and forever.

Jeff had some experience with closeted guys in countries where homosexuality is illegal, where young men fall instantly in love with older foreigners, so he played the game and replied with a quotation from Lauren Child, British children's author: "We were given: Two hands to hold. Two legs to walk. Two eyes to see. Two ears to listen. But why only one heart? Because the other was given to someone else. For us to find."

Nima was overwhelmed with joy. The only thing he needed now was a visa for this other heart.

3.4 Increased Libido at Seventy

When Antoine reached sixty, his lover put an end to their long-term relationship. They remained friends, but their relationship was more or less limited to a dim sum brunch once a month. To achieve some sexual gratification, Antoine began dropping by the gay sauna, which is not always the best cruising spot for seniors. His libido gradually decreased to where he could go without sex for almost a year.

But at seventy, there was a sudden revival, and Antoine found himself dreaming of the good old days. Financially stable, if not well off, he contacted a rent-men agency and engaged in one-hour sexual encounters for $250. When he moved into a seniors' residence in downtown Toronto, Canada, Antoine met a guy in his midsixties who introduced him to a free online dating service called Daddies & Sons. This was a dream come true, since Antoine had always been attracted to younger guys.

On the site were profiles of thousands of men looking for sex partners, dates, long-term relationships, or simply friends. Each had a username to the tune of Yourtoy2use, Curiouscarrot, Hornynow, Isucklongfatdick, Letsdothistoday, or Sexaholic. The slogans were usually quite direct: Anything possible; I aim to please on Thursday afternoons; Ready and willing, never done this before; No games, just fun; Chubby needs a daddy; Looking for much older.

Even when the sexual orientation line indicated straight, the member was often looking for men or couples of two men, no women. The profile photos were 50 to 60 percent cocks and assholes, and some even included masturbation videos. Antoine was surprised to see the extremely large number of young guys under forty-five looking for men in their sixties, seventies, and even eighties.

Antoine chose Gay1976 as his username—the year he came out. For his slogan, Antoine hesitated between "Oral Man-to-Man Pleasure" and "Rimming King." He opted for the shorter one, to be punchier and also to clearly announce his colors. Antoine knew that his profile text had to be well crafted, not too long, and enticing. After four drafts, he finally posted this:

> Affectionate, romantic bilingual (French-English) looking for a man with whom I can talk, cuddle, hug, and kiss before heading to the bedroom. A leader in bed, I like to caress your crotch in a jockstrap

(will lend you one), slap your buns in tight jeans, strip you naked, suck your cock slowly and firmly, gradually lick and chew your balls, and slide my tongue in your ass to rim you with frenzy. You are between twenty-five and forty-five, a little submissive, like dirty talk, and are either cut or uncut (I'm cut). The best you can offer me is your rosebud to rim.

Antoine's profile picture showed him in a bulging red jockstrap standing next to an enlarged poster of two guys in faded blue jeans and black leather chaps. In his gallery, he added two photos: one sitting in front of a meal with a glass of wine in his right hand, the other sitting on a sofa with two adorable dogs, Lilly and Bruno. In both pics, Antoine had a short white beard. No videos were included.

The first month, Antoine received a dozen messages, but almost half were from guys who only wanted to chat, so he removed the "dirty talk" phrase from his profile text. He was also proactive, leaving messages on the sites of white, black, and Asian guys, freely giving out his email address and even his phone number. That triggered a first encounter with a Caribbean guy who was not too well endowed but was very active in bed, followed by a married man with two kids who had never kissed a guy. Antoine was so excited to be the first. His only regret was that these meetings never went beyond the one-night stand—until Rick showed up.

At least ten emails were exchanged before Antoine accepted a meeting with Rick, fifty-nine. He had never had sex with a man in his late fifties, but accepted hosting Rick because the slim red-haired man enjoyed cuddling, kissing, and being rimmed. What he had not foreseen was Rick's fetish for cheeks, and bearded ones drove him crazy. Rick came on aggressively, squeezing Antoine's cheeks forcefully and kissing them passionately, but no kiss on the lips. A hop in the bedroom was a relief and a chance for Antoine to suck and rim this strange partner, who did not give him a hard-on.

In the course of their sexual romp, between a full-blown rod at one end and a delicious asshole at the other, Rick freely confided. He preferred to caress a soft cock rather than a hard dick, and no sucking. He liked to be rimmed but did not want to reciprocate. He enjoyed exploding in a guy's mouth. And most of all, he was ready to become Antoine's sex partner once a week.

After a light dinner—shrimp pasta salad and Henkell sparkling wine—they amicably parted after three big smacks on each of Antoine's cheeks. Antoine spent the rest of the night evaluating the situation, writing down the pros and cons of this possible relationship. It was a plus to suck and rim Rick, who received satisfaction by being rimmed and caressing a soft cock. Antoine could neither be sucked nor rimmed, and Rick could not explode in his partner's mouth. Antoine had a steady partner, and Rick could materialize his fetish of kissing bearded cheeks. The count was not perfectly equal, but Antoine told himself that at seventy, as Beckett said, "Perfection is not of this world."

3.5 The Enterprising Salesman in the Cubicle

arcel and Paul have met through an international dating site offering younger guys an opportunity to hook up with Silver Daddies. Marcel is a thirty-four-year-old guy from Ivory Coast who dreams of sucking a white cock. Paul is a seventy-one-year-old man from Canada who just wants to bury his face in a young black ass. They're a good match, but distance is a barrier.

Close friends of Paul have cautioned him to be prudent and realistic. What are the chances of meeting Marcel face-to-face, face-to-cock, face-to-ass? Pretty slim when you're 6,200 miles apart. But Paul has a tendency to fall in love with … love. He started by sending passionate emails, followed by romantic phone calls. He even wrote hardcore porn stories based on the nude pictures that his long-distance lover wholeheartedly agreed to send him.

If an African cock can be the size of a tusk, then Marcel is average, hung with an eight-inch weapon, cut and crowned by a huge knob that can easily spurt a full saucer of creamy white nectar. His rosebud is hairless, smooth, and mouthwatering. Paul has enlarged a picture of Marcel's chocolate starfish and hung it right next to his queen-size bed. When he's horny, he wears his red jockstrap, caresses his small pistol, winks at the puckered brown eye over his shoulder, and masturbates while chanting M-A-R-C-E-L. Instant explosion.

Marcel will turn thirty-five in one month. He's penniless and can't afford a tablet computer. What a golden opportunity for a birthday gift! Western Union in Toronto will send $350 Canadian, but headquarters blocks the transaction. What is the purpose of this transfer? How long have you known this man? Have you met him in person? Paul gets back his $350 and successfully applies to Money Gram.

Ever since he discovered his attraction toward young men, Paul has developed a tight jeans fetish. The sight of a guy's ass or crotch in faded blue denim easily triggers a hard-on. He dreams of seeing Marcel in skin-tight Levi's. When Levi Strauss invented rugged jeans with copper rivets at the pockets and fly for miners and lumberjacks in the early 1870s, he did not suspect that this garment would one day become a sensual envelope prized by homosexuals eager to exhibit their manhood.

After being washed and then dried in the sun, the jeans mold to the body and bring out a firm round ass, a generous mushroomed joystick, and a set of balls coiled at the top of the fork. No wonder the wearing of jeans has become a must in gay bars, discos, and cruising venues.

Another Money Gram transfer, another fifty-dollar gift, and Marcel can shop in Zuenoula, not too far from the capital city of Yamoussoukro. He rushes to a sportswear store and dons a pair of Levi's jeans in his size.

The salesman, who is fifty-five or sixty years old and rather handsome, with a small, round belly, looks Marcel over thoughtfully. "I think they're a bit loose," he says.

"You're probably right. I'll try a smaller size." Anticipation is apparent in Marcel's flushed cheeks.

"Let me help you," says the salesman, not hesitating to caress Marcel's buttocks. "They'll be a little difficult to put on, but I'm sure you'll be satisfied with the result," he adds, breathing more heavily as he lets his hand wander to Marcel's fly.

Marcel moans slightly with pleasure and looks at himself in the mirror with satisfaction.

"You should try them without your underwear. That's even more exciting," suggests the salesman.

"Can I do that here, without first paying for the jeans?" asked Marcel.

"With my permission," said the salesman, "and only if I accompany you into the cubicle."

Marcel gets naked, and the size of his dick amazes the salesman, who helps him put on the jeans. The touch of the rough fabric directly on his flesh makes Marcel's bazooka inflate, which again triggers a wandering hand. The salesman is now on his knees to check that everything falls nicely into place. He pats Marcel's butt, adds a firm squeeze, and drops a "Fuck, your back door is so appetizing!" Without losing any time, he pulls out his stiff dick and starts wanking it in Marcel's denim crack.

Marcel can't believe what's happening. The flesh-and-denim combination creates an exciting sensation, bringing his cock to stretch out to at least eight inches. When the salesman puts his mouth on the well-defined mushroom knob, Marcel can barely hold the sap of his tube. The salesman holds his client firmly, one hand on the butt, the other one on the balls. He bites the clothed dick and easily brings it to an explosion and a planned conclusion. "Now that your sperm has left traces on the fabric," says the salesman, "you have no choice but to buy these jeans."

Back home, Marcel washes his jeans and dries them in the sun a few times to get the denim softer and tighter. His buttocks and crotch definitely become more attractive. When Paul telephones at eight o'clock that night, his Ivorian is already excited. Paul loves it when his long-distance lover talks about a guy's ass, cock, balls, and anus, using terms like *back door*, *lunch box*, *purple-headed soldier*, *jellybean sack*, and *rosebud*. The Canadian and the Ivorian make love over the phone.

Marcel sends pictures of his bulging crotch draped in denim and his tightly wrapped hindquarters. The pair of jeans is the best birthday present—after the portable computer, of course! They are two outlets that keep the long-distance relationship alive and well.

3.6 Not So Polite and Gentle

I f I mention Finland, the name Tom pops up, right? Tom of Finland, of course, known for his highly masculinized fetish artworks. His real name is Touko Laaksonen, and his gay pornographic images feature mainly macho men with exaggerated cocks and muscled torsos and asses. They always have short hair and no beard, and they're often dressed in the uniform of a navy man, patrol police, jail officer, and so on.

When I met Matt, a twenty-six-year-old Finnish guy, at the bathhouse in downtown Toronto, I asked if he was a slutty Tom-of-Finland descendant. He immediately told me that his preference was Gengoroh Tagame.

Tagame is a Japanese manga artist noted for his works depicting graphic themes of sadomasochism, sexual violence, and hypermasculinity. He is celebrated around the world for his groundbreaking work, complete with masterful imagery and unbridled explorations of bondage, lust, passion, and romance. For him, violence is manly, and the experience of danger is exciting.

Don't get me wrong—Matt is not a violent or dangerous guy. He measures barely five foot seven and doesn't weigh more than 152 pounds, which is nothing to scare the hell out of you. He's known to be nice, polite, and gentle, but the other side of the coin is quite different. Matt likes to be tied up and raped by an aggressive dick or a darting tongue. Oh, I forgot to mention that my friend is a vegetarian, so if the cock is the size of an eggplant, and if the tongue is like an asparagus, then he's more than satisfied.

I'm known to have a sharp tongue in discussions, and even more in ass eating. My prowess was sharpened by the fact that Matt wore a jockstrap and that his ass was superbly draped with red, white, and blue waist and thigh elastics. I'm French, and I immediately saw the French flag that I had to honor, so to speak.

Matt and I ended up enjoying pillow talk, jumping from one subject to another, with a lick, a kiss, or a bite in between, frotting our dicks as soon as they started to rise. I found out that Matt has a fetish for men in uniforms. Security guards in their fifties rank pretty high.

"I sometimes indulge in small shoplifting just to have a security guard run after me," he told me.

"And what happens if he catches you?" I asked.

"We end up in a back room, where I plead distraction. I discreetly brush my knee against his crotch and naively smile, and then he starts to grab my jewels. You know what I mean—not a cheap bracelet or necklace, but the real lottery prize!"

"Amazing!" I exclaimed. "And he ends up fucking you?"

Matt said, "Not so fast. I tell him that I deserve to be punished, that I want to be tied naked to a warehouse post and spanked in a manly fashion."

"Which is one way of saying that you long to be beaten by his stiff rod?" I asked.

"How did you guess?"

"You're a fucking little pervert, Matt, inspired by Gengoroh Tagame's filthy mind."

"Indeed, I adore being humiliated, beaten, tortured, raped, and pleasured by an older man in a uniform."

I quickly learned that Matt's definition of *uniform* was pretty broad. It included, for example, the white, green, or blue medical clothing worn by dentists. At first, when he had an appointment with the paternal Dr. Benson, Matt took pleasure in having the dentist stick a thick finger in his mouth, but he was too shy to make a move. So I told him, "Listen, Matt, no risk, no trick!" Now my friend moans with pleasure while nonchalantly brushing his right elbow against the dentist's crotch. This inevitably triggers a bulge and an instant reaction. Dr. Benson locks the door, shuts the blinds, pulls out his extra tool, and attacks Matt's wide-open mouth.

A violent behavior of that nature is exactly what my friend dreams about when he's flipping through the pages of Gengoroh Tagame's graphic novel *Endless Game*. Dr.

Benson has become a vivid depiction of the mangaka's erotic pulsing. By now, Matt's one-eyed trouser snake has sneaked out of its jockstrap and made a "coming out" in the dentist chair. While fucking his patient's brain, Dr. Benson strangles the snake and gives Matt a brutal jerk-off. They both sense that their volcanoes are ready to erupt, and when they explode, Matt can't refrain from screaming "Holy fuck" at the top of his two heads: skull and mushroom!

The receptionist feels sorry for him. "Why is Dr. Benson hurting such a polite and gentle guy?"

4

Russian and Ukrainian File

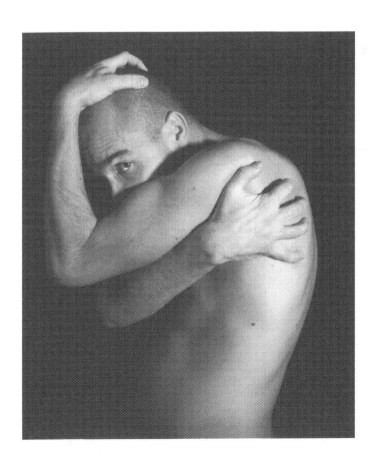

4.1　Two Lovebirds in Orenburg

For the previous thirty years, Jean-Pierre had always visited a different country at the end of the summer. In 2018, however, he changed his routine and decided to return to Russia. A touring company had asked him to write a series of articles on Orenburg, southeast of Moscow on the boundary between Europe and Asia. Jean-Pierre was planning to describe the habitat of species along the Ural River: Dalmatian pelican, greater flamingo, squacco heron, short-toed eagle, and whooper swan.

His plans changed, however, when he arrived at the Stepnaya Palmira Hotel. As he walked toward the registration desk, a twenty-five-year-old handsome guy with a "Stay Hungry for Creativity, Inspiration & Art" T-shirt winked at him and briefly disappeared—only to reappear five minutes later in a dress shirt with a name tag that read "Aleksandr." He took Jean-Pierre's information, smiled intriguingly, and gave him the key and a welcoming handshake.

The smiling clerk then approached closely and

whispered that it was a practice at that hotel to make sure the client was satisfied with his room. "In two hours, I will knock to ensure that you are comfortably installed, sir."

Since there was a nine-hour difference between Toronto and Orenburg, Jean-Pierre took a little nap after unpacking. He kept thinking of Aleksandr's smile, manly deodorant, and virile look. An hour later, Jean-Pierre showered, dressed casually, and feverishly waited for the knock on the door, which was smooth and gentle. When Aleksandr walked in, he was carrying a tray with a bottle of champagne, two glasses, a plate of Swiss cheese and baguette, a bowl of cashew nuts, and fresh fruits.

The hotel knew that the Canadian guest was a writer and would no doubt mention the hotel in his article, so a welcoming bang was in order. Jean-Pierre was more intrigued by the hotel clerk's attitude than by the appetizing platter.

"Can I invite you for a drink after my shift, sir?" asked Aleksandr.

"Of course, but call me JP. I have a travel budget for such expenses, so I'll pay for the drinks."

"Very nice of you, my first Canadian guest. I do not want to impose, but maybe you would prefer to come to my place and have a more friendly welcome party …"

"That's a great idea, my son— oh, I mean, my new Russian friend."

"Call me Sasha. It is more intimate, sir— I mean, JP."

"Can I embrace you, handsome Sasha?"

The two men were energized and hugged firmly. JP tried to hide his bulging crotch, but Sasha just smiled and reciprocated with a kiss on the lips.

"I have to go back to the front desk," said Sasha. "Meet me at eight o'clock this evening on the steps of the hotel, my king."

"You can count on me, my prince."

JP took a map at the front desk, smiled at Sasha, and was off for a quick tour of some iconic attractions, the most touristic one being the pedestrian bridge between Europe and Asia. Photos of the water tower and the Sculpture Sarmatskiy Olen were also a must, plus a short orientation tour of the Regional Fine Arts Museum, to be explored more thoroughly later in the week.

The meeting on the steps of Stepnaya Palmira Hotel was refreshing and exhilarating. After just one turn on the next street, JP tried to hold Sasha's hand, but he was quickly reminded of a sociocultural difference in Russia. However, he didn't have to wait long, because Sasha lived close by, and as soon as his apartment door was closed, the men kissed passionately.

They cuddled on the love seat, whispering tender words of trust and bonding. JP found Sasha to be astoundingly sure of himself. The age difference was no barrier to a deep expression of emotions. Sasha had obviously prepared himself for this close encounter. His well-crafted poem could finally reach its climax:

You are my gentle, beloved, dear person.
I appreciate you, I adore you.
With all my heart, I love you!
You are my king, you are my ideal.
The Lord sent you to me as a reward.
Be the sweet sun that will enlighten my life.
I am happy with you. Do you hear, my dear?
You are sent by heaven to me, by fate.
Always be healthy, successful,
And with me always be gentle.
May our dreams come true.
The best in this world is you!

Sasha then guided JP to his bedroom, slowly undressing him to cuddle again, but in all the splendor of a full-blown tower of virile beauty. Each kiss became a breath of love. Each caress went beyond the erotic body to reach the inner soul, the heart.

That first night, JP did not try to go further down the road of lust. The romantic Canadian tourist knew that he would sleep with Sasha for the next week. He just dreamed of embracing him emotionally and sexually for the rest of his life.

4.2 New Canada-Russia Relations

E very year, in a small Russian town near St. Petersburg, patrons of the arts organize a visual art competition. In 2019, young artists were invited to draw a man's body inspired by a short story by a fifty-nine-year-old Canadian guest writer. His name was Paul-François, and his chosen story had a direct homoerotic tone.

At first the patrons' decision to invite a gay writer caused a scandal, since homosexuality is seen by a majority of Russian citizens as a disease. Some would even go so far as *ubijstva chesti*—honor killing—to protect the family from the shame a gay son would bring. But this writer was a foreigner and had a visa, so the competition went ahead as planned.

A handsome male artist named Stanislav, with a cute round face and sweet red lips, was the first to register for the competition. Stanislav's mother had encouraged him to draw since he was six years old. His high school art teacher knew that Stas had a promising talent that just needed to be nurtured. He also knew that Stas was different, more sensitive than most guys, so he supported the young artist with kind words and taps on the shoulder—though he would have preferred to tap his firm round butt.

Paul-François arrived a week before the competition and met the young artists who had registered, to elaborate on the characters portrayed in the selected short story. During the discussion Stanislav suddenly had an idea, but he decided to wait and raise it in private with the author.

When Paul-François and Stanislav later met for coffee, the young artist said, "Thank you for agreeing to coach me, Mr. François."

"Call me Paul. We have a lot in common, I think."

"I was wondering if I could draw a portrait of the author, instead of a picture of the main character in the short story."

"Well, that's an original idea, my handsome young man!" exclaimed Paul. "Would you want me to pose? And where could we do that?"

"I draw at home, in my room. I see no other place. Does that bother you, Paul?"

"Absolutely not. We can start now if you want."

Stanislav had chores to do for his mother, but he jumped at the opportunity, knowing that his mom would understand. The author and the young artist, both trembling with excitement, took their places behind closed doors in Stanislav's small bedroom.

Paul had been through a similar experience in his

own country, and he knew the best approach to make his student feel more comfortable. "One works best, Stanislav, when one feels natural."

"What do you mean, Paul?"

"Our bodies are naturally naked. We are not born wearing clothing."

"Are you suggesting that we remove our clothes for this portrait session?"

"That would be natural, not to say inspiring. Don't you think so, my handsome Stanislav?"

"I agree, my dear Paul, and you can call me Stas."

Once naked, author and artist felt energized and drawn toward each other. Paul held Stas's face in his warm hands, blew a kiss to it, and triggered a passionate embrace. Stas's hands were still trembling, so he held tightly to Paul, who did not hesitate to give him a French kiss. This set in motion another form of art: a man-to-man ballet in which the choreography could have been scripted by Rudolph Nureyev.

Each step was an homage to virility. Each cock grew in size and led the two lovers to take their places on the narrow bed. Their natural desires had no limit. Paul licked just about every inch of Stas's body, culminating in sucking his superhard uncut dick, almost chewing the marvelous pink mushroom. Stas was moaning with pleasure, and he reciprocated in like manner. Paul's dick was delicious, but his ass was even more inviting, so Stas plunged his tongue into it with urgency. He had never rimmed anyone, and this excited him so much that he paused to yell his pleasure.

Paul had never felt so good. "Oh yes, Stas, suck my rosette, you little demon!"

"I also want to fuck your divine ass, my gorgeous Paul."

"It's all yours. Enjoy fully!"

Stas gently inserted his naturally lubricated cock into Paul's rosette and then gradually started to pump the firm rod. The choreography climaxed with an explosion of nectar. The artist and the writer had heaven on earth, the *summum bonum*, or highest good.

The young artist's drawing of a fifty-nine-year-old man's face intrigued the jury, who recognized that the art expressed both energy and serenity. It did not win first prize, but as a form of encouragement, the jury invited Stanislav for a short trip to St. Petersburg and the Hermitage Museum.

In the museum, Stas was directed to a gallery where he could admire many portraits of men. Rembrandt's bearded man reminded Stas of Paul's photo.

A guide named Igor, in his early sixties, approached Stas with a particular interest. "You will certainly like Franz Kruger's portrait of Fersen."

"Why, sir?" asked Stas. "Does it have a special feature?"

"It is almost a portrait of you. Fersen is as handsome as you are, young man."

Stas was astonished by the resemblance. He approached

closely, almost eye to eye, but when he crossed the line on the floor, Igor pulled him back—brushing his hand against Stas's butt and smiling lustfully.

Stas followed the guide from one painting to another, often feeling Igor's hand on his shoulder, at his waist, on his thigh, even wandering down to his butt. There was erotic electricity in the air, and no one else was around, so Igor surprised Stas with a quick kiss.

"Your lips are so sweet," said the guard.

"Thank you, sir," Stas replied. "You're a very attractive man."

"Call me Igor. What's your name?"

"Stanislas, but you can call me Stas."

"Would you like to visit the secret gallery, not open to the public?"

"Wow! That would be great," said Stas.

They exited through a secret door and ended up in a small room that looked like an artist's studio. An unfinished painting of a nude man got them both excited. It was Pablo Picasso's sketch of *Nude Figure of Young Man*. Inviting Stas to sit on the sofa next to the sketch, Igor embraced him tenderly. Stas responded with a penetrating wet kiss and pulled down Igor's pants. The guide's dick was now as hard as a large paintbrush handle.

Igor slowly undressed Stas, who spontaneously showed his rising virility. "You have a gorgeous phallus, my handsome dude."

"Thanks, Igor. Can I suck your long hard cock?"

"Of course! Why not taste each other's jewels in a sixty-nine position?"

They lost no time in giving each other oral pleasure. Sensing that they were close to cumming, they both had the same reflection at the same time—sliding their tongue on the balls, licking the ass crack, and reaching the rosebud, which they rimmed eagerly. When Stas's asshole was well lubricated with saliva, Igor penetrated him, slowly at first but gradually pounding the young man's divine hemisphere. Another episode of *summum bonum.*

4.3 Mutual Attraction in the Park

Toronto was burning bright under the spring sun, and the last patches of snow had melted. After the exercise program at his seniors' residence, Paul decided to go for a walk and ended up in St. James Park. The daffodils were in full bloom, and the tulips were burgeoning. But above all this, Paul noticed a young guy approaching him. He smiled and continued to walk slowly, but then turned around to see that the cute dude had also turned around. They were drawn to each other.

"Would you like to sit down and chat with an old man?" asked Paul.

"You're not an old man—you're a mature and handsome man."

"Thank you. And what is the name of this cute pink face with sweet red lips?"

"My name is Yurochka, but you can call me Yuri. I'm a Russian tourist in an organized group visiting Canada, and we have this afternoon free. What's your name?"

"I'm Paul, born in this province, Ontario, and I'm a writer."

Yuri asked, "Do you write love poems, Paul?"

"No, I prefer short stories of men loving men. I think you also like that, right?"

"Yes, one hundred percent, but in Russia gays are not well treated. It can be quite dangerous."

"Here you can live openly, kiss in public, even get married legally. How old are you, Yuri?"

"I'm twenty-nine, but I don't have much experience with men. And you, Paul, you look like fifty."

"I'm fifty-nine, in fact, and I have a lot of experience that I'm willing to share with handsome dudes like you," Paul said, putting his hand on Yuri's thigh and exerting light pressure.

Yuri smiled and sat closer to Paul. An electro-sexual shock occurred, and each man felt a jolt in the groin. Paul preferred younger guys with whom he could initiate and dominate the sex. Losing no time, he invited Yuri to his apartment. *This young guy has an angelic face, but he will become a sexy demon in my arms*, thought Paul.

As soon as they entered the penthouse loft, Yuri noticed the homoerotic pictures on the wall. Paul obviously had a fetish for guys in jockstraps, tight faded jeans, leather gear, and even rubber. Yuri was glad that he had worn his blue jeans, which were getting tighter because of a growing bulge. Paul invited him to cuddle on the love seat and slowly started to kiss him—Canadian embrace, Russian moans of pleasure.

Paul whispered a suggestion in Yuri's ear, softly biting it. The reaction was a green light for the bedroom. "You can call me Daddy," he said.

Yuri asked, "Do you see me as your son?"

"No, more like my godson."

"Thank you for such a hot compliment. You can do what you want with me, Daddy."

Daddy brushed crotch to crotch with his godson, then grabbed his firm round ass in his blue jeans and started to spank it lightly. Yuri was taken aback at first—he had never imagined this, but he found it erotic. Daddy slapped a little harder in the groin, triggering three supplications from his adorable Russian partner: "Can you lick me? Can you suck me? Can you fuck me?"

The king-size bed had now become an arena of man-to-man pleasure, an altar of virility. Paul and Yuri both undressed, kissed again, and positioned themselves for a hot sixty-nine encounter.

"I really like your uncut dick. It is so nice to see the pink mushroom come out at the tip of your hard rod."

"Can I cum in your mouth, Dad?"

"Not yet, son. First I want to rim you."

"What's that?"

It was not surprising that Yuri knew nothing about anilingus or anal-oral contact, since rimming ranks down the list at thirty-four among the most popular sexual practices in Russia. Paul initiated him like a pro, explaining the term *rosette*, or rosebud. When his son was ready to explode, Daddy ordered him to hold a second or two because he wanted to drink the banana juice. In fact, when they were both back to the sixty-nine position, a succulent fruit salad was on the menu, including the traditional cherry.

The Canada-Russia exchange was not over yet. Paul and Yuri cuddled on the bed, embraced warmly, and kissed passionately, after which the young Russian proudly exhibited another hard-on. This time, Paul wanted the whole glorious rod up his ass.

"It's now your turn to rim me, son. Get my rosette real wet with your tongue, then stick your gun in it. I'm ready for a hold-up!"

"I've never done this before, Dad, but I'm willing to learn."

"You look and sound like an angel, but I know that you're a gay demon deep inside."

No sooner said than done. Yuri hadn't known that a clean but sweaty shit hole could smell and taste so good. It energized his rod, and encouraged by Paul, he spit on his firm dick before shoving it in Paul's tight asshole, slowly at first, then powerfully. In no time, Paul was hearing what sounded like a foreign language, no doubt Russian words: "Черт, это так хорошо!" He did not need to ask for a translation, because Yuri alternated with "Fuck, this is so good!"

4.4　The Power of Words and Dreams

Egor is a handsome twenty-four-year-old Russian guy. Blond, brown eyes, medium build—five foot six and 143 pounds. He keeps fit by going to the gym and taking long walks in the parks of Samara. The city is in the southeastern part of Russia, at the confluence of the Volga and Samara Rivers. Across the Volga River are the Zhiguli Mountains, after which the local beer, Zhigulyovskoye, is named.

Samara's riverfront is one of the favorite recreation places for local citizens and tourists. Egor works as a guide during the summer months and sometimes as a lifeguard on the beach. The average temperature in July and August is around 77 degrees Fahrenheit, but it can rise to more than 85 or even 95 degrees. When Egor supervises the beach, he is often distracted by luscious nude men sunbathing, which gives him a bulging crotch that he tries to hide with his towel.

At the end of his shift, Egor always takes a shower and is followed by well-endowed older men who nonchalantly exhibit their manhood. As soon as he's alone with an entrepreneurial man, Egor lets him soap his back and his butt, which brings the man to his knees, eager to suck Egor's long, hard uncut dick. His chopper mushroom can be quite juicy.

Egor is attracted to men twice his age, even much older, but the men he meets on the beach are always married and interested only in a quick sexual encounter. In 2012 Samara had seven gay clubs, but now there is only one very discreet venue opposite a row of garages. No sign of a nightclub, no queue, no music or crowds of smokers spilling out into the street. Not a place where Egor wants to go.

In recent years, Samara has been dubbed the most homophobic city in the country. It isn't illegal to practice homosexuality in Russia, but promoting the gay "lifestyle" is a crime—and what constitutes promotion is at the discretion of the authorities. In this context, Egor turned to an international gay online dating site called Man Nation, where he easily hooked up with Michael. The Canadian writer could be his grandfather, but Egor doesn't believe that age is the most important thing in a relationship.

Michael writes erotic short stories for Gay Demon, a Swedish porn site that attracts close to fifty thousand visitors a day. He sends a few of his stories to Egor, including two based on correspondence he had with gay guys in Orenburg and St. Petersburg.

Egor replies immediately, "Thank you so much. I read your stories. That was great. I was very excited. And my dick became hard as a brick." Egor goes on to say that he loves to fuck a man and enjoys having his dick sucked. "But I also like to suck a man who cums in my mouth—wow!"

For a writer, this kind of comment is very rewarding. Michael remembers signing his new gay novel, *The Unloved*, at a book fair. The next day, one guy came back to say, "I read your novel in one night. I really identified with the main character. It made me feel proud to be gay." Michael was touched, and he told his publisher that even if he had written *The Unloved* just for that one man, it would have been well worth it.

Egor and Michael communicate every other day by email, and they exchange photos. At first it's family pictures, but Michael gradually persuades his Russian correspondent to send more intimate material. To set the tone, he emails pics of his cock and hairy asshole. Egor adores them, writing back to say that he now dreams of sucking a Canadian's cock and fucking the ass that goes with it. In Russia, gay dreams are part of a daily reality.

Through one of his stories titled "The Art of Tongue Dancing," Michael initiates Egor into rimming, explaining that a tongue inside a guy's anus can drive him wild. "Unlike the head of your penis," he says, "your anus rarely gets sore or oversensitized from use. I've met some men who were so relaxed that I managed to work my entire tongue all the way inside, driving the quietest of them to yell out, 'Oh God! Oh fuck!'"

Within their first month of exchanges, Michael crafts a short story just for Egor's eyes and pleasure.

In fact, that's not exactly true. "The Power of Words and Dreams" is now available to thousands of readers, thanks to Gay Demon.

4.5 Tongue-Twisting My Pleasure

Alex is a thirty-five-year-old gym trainer born in Ukraine. He's five foot nine and weighs 187 pounds. Though his body is firmly toned, he doesn't look macho like Arnold Schwarzenegger because he's always smiling. No doubt, he's a handsome Mr. Muscle who has the gift of energizing both men and women. Ukrainian society is quite homophobic, so no one knows that Alex is gay, not even his mother or sister, both of whom also work in the fitness industry.

Contrary to what you would expect from a bodybuilder, Alex likes to write poems and read romantic novels, and he enjoys the music of the Red Hot Chili Peppers, Bryan Adams, and Madonna. He has not yet found his other half, but it will likely be a man at least thirty years older who enjoys oral sex. Alex is not much into anal gratification. He prefers cuddling, kissing, sucking, and rimming. The latter drives him crazy, and a tongue is the only tool he needs to sculpt his man-to-man pleasure.

To earn an international certificate in CrossFit training, Alex has to spend a few months in Toronto, Canada. His program includes competitive fitness sports as well as physical exercises incorporating gymnastics, Olympic weightlifting, kettlebell lifting, power lifting, and high-intensity interval training. Not surprisingly, Alex's arms, shoulders, pecs, thighs, and butt are cast in iron.

When he arrives in late June at his Airbnb near the GoodLife Fitness club and gym in downtown Toronto, Alex is met by Paul, sixty-eight, who just feels like melting in his client's arms. Paul gives Alex a warm, welcoming hug and a discreet but firm tap on the butt. Alex smiles and tries to hide his suddenly bulging crotch, but Paul is quick to notice that they're on the same wavelength.

Meals are not included in the Airbnb package, but Paul often invites Alex to share a dinner. He introduces the Ukranian to lobster rolls, stuffed avocado with crabmeat, and poutine, a dish composed of French fries, cheese curds, and gravy. Alex regularly offers to cook Ukrainian dishes such as borscht, *golubtsi*, *draniki*, *pelmeni*, and *galushki*. A liter of wine accompanies these brotherly feasts every Friday night, and Alex always ends up relaxing on the burgundy leather sofa.

The men are always in a merry mood, and sometimes slightly intoxicated. Cannabis has just been legalized in Canada for recreational purposes, so Paul and Alex enjoy their 4:20 at 9:20, easily cuddling and giggling. Paul usually takes the lead in pressing a hand on his guest's thigh or even sliding a finger across his nipples. Like Paul, Alex is a Capricorn and a leader. He doesn't hesitate to caress his host's short-trimmed beard and press his earlobe. This triggers a kiss and an embrace, and they melt in each other's arms.

"Alex, you often say that you like meat. I have the perfect dish, and it comes with a mushroom."

"Mine comes with meatballs, Paul."

"We're in for a double treat, my friend."

On that note, Paul and Alex head for the master bedroom. They don't have to say a word, because they both want to enjoy oral pleasure. At sixty-eight, Paul's diabetes causes him erectile problems. He likes to suck a cock but does not easily get a hard-on, but this isn't a cause for concern, because rimming is at the top of their list. Alex takes the first step by kissing Paul's butt and slapping it mildly before burying his face in the divine crack, drooling over it, smelling the manly odor, and starting to suck the hairy rosebud enthusiastically. Paul moans with pleasure, which encourages Alex to tongue-twist his entrance into the satanic haven, triggering a loud, "Fuck, you are amazing! This is divine!"

Roles are naturally inverted and Paul now has the surprise of smelling Alex's sweaty gym odor, which beats any fragrance from Hugo Boss, Burberry, Versace, Calvin Klein, Lagerfeld, or D&G. Alex's rear end is hairless, firm, and shiny. For Paul, it's like holding and adoring Rodin's

The Age of Bronze. His short beard tickles Alex's prized possession and makes him giggle. As soon as Paul darts his tongue to reach his partner's arsehole—which he prefers to call the crinkled star or even the leather Cheerio—Alex begs, "Bang my rump like a punching ball. Chew my bunghole like a pelmeni. This is pure delight!"

After their trip down Pleasure Lane, Paul and Alex feel like they're floating on a cloud. They sleep in each other's arms, and in the morning Paul serves coffee and pancakes with maple syrup. "I'm going to rent out your room as of today," he says. "You're moving in with me, free of charge, but you have to guarantee a tongue-twisting pleasure on demand."

The reply is quick and decisive: "You can count on me and my oral talent."

5
American File

5.1 Casino Fever

Paul didn't usually frequent casinos, but since he had free time in Niagara Falls, Canada, he told himself that one hour behind a slot machine couldn't hurt. *Who knows? I might have beginner's luck*, he thought. In fact, he was going to be a lucky daddy!

As he sat down in front of a three sevens machine, he noticed a young man actively pumping his crazy diamonds machine. What Paul noticed, to be honest, were the muscular biceps of his neighbor, the firm torso of this handsome dude, and the tight jean shorts he was wearing. Since Paul had a jeans and jockstrap fetish, he imagined this young virile hunk playing in a red jockstrap. That got him horny, but what could he do in a public area? Social contact was the first step.

"Hi, my name is Paul."

"Hi, Paul, my name is Jeff and I'm American. Are you Canadian?"

"Yes, French Canadian. Any luck so far?"

"Two steps forward, one step backward."

"The nice grin on your face seems to show some satisfaction …"

"Hope you'll smile too, Paul. No need to be serious here."

"You're right, Jeff. In fact, I feel more like watching you play. Mind if I sit next to you? Might bring you some luck." Paul stood and approached Jeff hesitantly.

Jeff smiled warmly and slouched over slightly. "That's a good idea, Paul. Please sit close to me. I'll imagine that you're a daddy putting an arm around his son's shoulders." Jeff seemed to brace himself.

Not losing a second, Paul took his place as close as possible to Jeff. They both smiled, and Paul felt Jeff's knee lightly brush against his thigh. Was that a sign?

"You energize me, handsome daddy," the smooth-skinned Jeff said, his flesh seeming to warm under Paul's embrace. Jeff gripped Paul's hand and pressed it warmly.

Paul felt relief, but he also felt heat within. "Feels so good, my virile son."

"Do you have something in mind?" Jeff asked.

Paul replied, "Plenty of fun, to be honest."

"Same here, Daddy. Do you have a hotel room?"

"Yes, and it's waiting for you, Sonny," said Paul.

"Great. Let's go!"

In no time at all, Paul and Jeff were cuddling on the room's love seat. Daddy could feel his son's crotch bulging, which triggered a passionate embrace and an exchange of deep wet kisses. Daddy then grabbed his son's firm ass and started to massage it, even slap it lightly.

"Oh yes, Daddy, give me a spanking," said Jeff.

Paul asked, "Have you been a naughty boy?"

"Not naughty, just horny!"

"I can help you with that, sonny boy. I order you to strip down."

"Yes, sir," said Jeff. "I offer you my thick pink dick."

"And your sweet rosette also?"

"What is a rosette, Daddy?"

Paul explained, "It's your asshole, which I want to lick, suck, and rim!"

"Wow, you taught me a new word, and it's so poetic. Thank you, Daddy."

In no time they were lying on top of each other on the king-size bed. Daddy sucked his son's long hard stick and chewed his testicles, which were as big as golf balls. Moans of satisfaction pushed Daddy to increase this pleasure by sliding his tongue into his new son's crack, reaching the rosebud with excitement. His tongue acted like a bee darting a flower to suck the nectar.

Ever since he was a teenager, Paul had placed virility on an altar. He now had a monument of masculinity that he could worship wholeheartedly. Daddy did not lose time and, with his tongue and two hands, brought his son to climax.

Jeff was as active as Paul. He had dreamed of venerating a daddy, and now all the stars were aligned.

He sucked Daddy's succulent mushroom until it gave him a warm soup and cries of pure joy.

"Can son fuck Daddy?" Jeff asked.

"Your rod is too thick," said Paul. "You'll hurt me."

Jeff said, "I'm a gentle and caring son. Please trust me, Holy Father."

"Oh! When I was a child, I wanted to become a priest, and now you can make me a pope. Okay, but go smoothly."

Son whispered tender words in Daddy's ear, bent him over, and started to slide his rod in the crack, getting it harder and harder as Daddy breathed heavily. Son had no KY or Crisco, so he used his saliva to lubricate Daddy's rosette, then finger-fucked him. When he heard him shout, "Fuck, I had no idea it could be this divine!" he shoved his rod in and pounded his new holy father gently.

It was the beginning of a long Canada-US relationship.

5.2 The Horny Alaskan

Josh is a thirty-five-year-old healthy guy who lives in Alaska. At five foot ten and 162 pounds, he has a toned body, firm round butt, muscular thighs and biceps, curly black hair, brown eyes, and a trimmed mustache. Did I forget to mention that Josh is well endowed? His nickname is Stallion! Long, thick, cut, dark, pumping veins, huge violet mushroom—a dream come true for any avid cocksucker or hungry ass. He drives a Dodge Ram 1500 cab truck, and when he selected his license plates, he chose "HORNY."

My friend Josh works in a small warehouse with four other men roughly his own age. The boss is a fifty-year-old black man who has no hang-ups about sexual diversity. He's officially straight, but that remains to be verified. As for Josh, he's openly gay and wears overalls with a worn hole in the back seat. No underwear—just a sweaty black jockstrap that nicely frames a welcoming bubble butt.

The last time I spoke with Josh, he told me that when he's home alone and in need of man-to-man pleasure, he leaves the door open, starts playing with his favorite toy, a dildo, and nine out of ten times a curious Italian bi neighbor sneaks in to offer the real thing, a burgeoning salami.

An early bird, Josh takes a shower, grabs a cup of coffee, and heads for the warehouse. He's the first employee to arrive at the loading dock, where trucker Hank is already parked, a grin on his face.

"My partner couldn't make it this morning," says Hank, "so you'll have to help me unload thirty-eight boxes."

Josh replies, "You know that there's a price to pay for an extra hand, you little cockteaser!"

"Of course," Hank replies. "Why do you think I'm so early?"

"Good! Bend over. My plonker is ready to unload its junk in your trunk."

Hank is a black guy, and his white Calvin Klein briefs are like a shining moon. Josh slaps the two hemispheres, slides his hand between the legs, grabs the covered balls, and squeezes them to make Hank beg for action. He then tears a strategic hole in his briefs, lubricates his bazooka, and shoves it in like a trucker honking to the tune of, "Damn it, move ahead!" And that's precisely what Josh intends to do—move at a pounding pace until explosion.

Once the merchandise is unloaded, Josh and his coworker Ted quickly distribute it on the pads in the warehouse. They finish twenty minutes under the allotted time, and then they're free to do what they want. Slightly overweight, Ted is a bit out of breath, but every time he sees Josh bending down, the hole in Josh's overalls gradually boosts his libido. Finally Ted corners his coworker and orders him to pull them down; the sight of a hairy white ass framed in a black jockstrap triggers an immediate hard-on.

Ted quickly finds out that Josh's pooper is nicely lubricated. *That fucking fag has already written the script! Well, I'm going to execute it in such a way that I will blow his mind.* Ted pours a few drops of mechanical oil on his boner and saddles Josh, crying out loud, "We'll see who's the real stallion!" The door of the warehouse is not closed, and the black boss happens to walk by, hearing this unusual cry. He enters and follows the sound of increasingly luscious moans of pleasure.

Ted's dick has no stallion status. In fact, it's barely an asparagus compared with the boss's chocolate parsnip. And Josh's caboose can certainly handle two vegetables for lunch. On that note, the boss joins Ted to double-fuck Josh, whose swamp ass is more than willing to accommodate two drillers, no matter their size. To say that the pleasure reaches divine proportions is not an exaggeration. The holy trinity is a pale embodiment of what ass, penis, and balls can create together.

"Goddammit, Satan has taken possession of me, and no twin angels can screw as wide and deep as my two fucking buddies!" Josh screams.

5.3 Friendly Canada-USA Relations

In the city of Laguna Hills, California, Beckenham Park attracts not only families with kids but also older people in search of shade in the summer or some other interesting distraction. On weekends, the picnic tables and sports field are fully occupied, as well as the walkways. One Saturday afternoon in August, on one of these walkways, two senior men crossed each other's paths. Both turned and looked back, hoping to see the other's ass, but their eyes met instead. They smiled, and the more slender one, accustomed to the comings and goings in the park, immediately knew that the other man was a tourist.

"Are you visiting Laguna Hills?" he inquired.

"Yes. How did you know?"

"Oh, I noticed the Canadian flag on your belt pouch. I'm Kent."

"Nice to meet you, Kent. I'm Paul."

"Welcome, Paul! Would you like to join me for a coffee?"

"Yes, but maybe a lemonade for me," replied Paul.

Paul followed one step behind Kent, to admire his firm butt highlighted in blue spandex. He had always been attracted to men in tight stretchy pants. He sensed that Kent's invitation could go further than just a drink, and his dream was closer than he thought. Kent stopped at the fountain for a sip of water, and when it was Paul's turn to bend down, he felt a caressing hand on his butt. They both smiled again.

Paul said, "I have a room at the Hills Hotel and a complimentary bottle of sparkling wine. It would be better than coffee or lemonade, don't you think?"

"Good idea!" exclaimed Kent. "I accept your invitation, Paul, but I'll first call my partner to let him know that I'll be home a little later."

Kent had an open relationship with an Asian lover. The rule was usually "Don't ask, don't tell," but one time they had both entered a bathhouse, come out an hour later with their flame of the moment, and headed home to engage in their first foursome experience. Kent could not resist confiding that it had been three times more fun for each of them.

As soon as the Canadian and American dudes entered the hotel room, Paul suggested that they take a shower together. "But I first want to caress your bulging spandex crotch. It really turns me on."

Kent could not agree more. He let Paul enjoy his fetish and undressed him before joining his new friend under a large square shower nozzle. As they soaped each other's back, ass, and crotch, their hard dicks kept jolting nicely.

Paul noticed that Kent was wearing a cock ring, making his testicles look like two big golf balls. He immediately knelt down in front of this divine offering, slowly but firmly sucking the pink mushroom and squeezing the two meatballs.

"I'm sixty-nine years old," said Kent, "and sixty-nine is a magic number."

Paul replied, "I know, my handsome Yankee. Let's transform the bed into a shrine of masculinity."

They positioned themselves to have a mouthwatering fiesta. While tasting Kent's lunch, Paul squeezed his partner's firm butt and triggered moans of pleasure. He deduced that Kent would love a long, thorough rimming and tongue-fucking session.

Kent confirmed that deduction immediately. "I love having my ass played with. And if you also play with my nipples, I'll do whatever you ask. I enjoy being a total sub!"

As a leader in bed, Paul couldn't dream of a more exhilarating moment. Kent's asshole was the most beautiful rosette he had ever seen. On the spur of the moment, Paul choreographed a three-move ballet performance: pinch the nipples, bite the balls, dart the rosette. Or slap the ass, chew the nipples, and finger-fuck the American butt offered on a silver plate.

Kent was constantly shouting cries of satisfaction.

"Fucking good! Never had so much fucking fun! You are my fucking Royal Canadian Mounted Dude!" He was referring to the Royal Canadian Mounted Police, a federal police force active in all provinces and territories. What he liked the most about the RCMP agents was their high black leather boots, red jackets, and large brown-brimmed hats. Mounted on horses, these emblematic Canadian men were always so sexy. To him, RCMP meant Royal Canadian Manly Pleasure!

Kent imagined Paul dressed as a mounted policeman who suddenly became submissive, almost begging for an outlaw gangster to play with his ass, smell the raunchy aroma, and rim the Canadian rosebud. He didn't need an order, but mounted Paul like a rutting dog.

"I believe in friendly Canada-USA relations," said Kent.

"More than friendly, my tasty fucking Yankee!"

5.4 A Tale of Dirty Talk

O nce upon a time, a horny older man met a handsome young dude who fell under his spell. The older Canadian man's name was Paul, the American guy was called Jeff, and they enjoyed an irresistible mutual attraction. Paul lived in a penthouse condo in downtown Toronto overlooking Lake Ontario, so he invited Jeff for a drink—and more, if Jeff wanted. Jeff smiled and followed the good-looking bearded man, in whom he saw a possible daddy.

As soon as they were on the sofa, Jeff looked around and admired all the virile pictures on the walls. He appreciated the ones showing a senior in a jockstrap kissing a junior in tight, faded jeans.

"Can I call you Daddy?" he whispered in Paul's ear.

"Of course, my little son of a bitch!"

"Oh, I really like dirty talk. Please continue," said Jeff.

"You're in for a surprise, Sonny. Dirty talk and dirty fun!"

The two cuddled, and Daddy lost no time in kissing

his hot new sex toy. "I worship virility, and I'm the priest of masculinity," he declared. "You're going to be my little fucking altar boy!"

Jeff said, "Your wish is my command, Holy Father! Do what you have to do so I can have heaven on earth."

"Great! I see that you are wearing tight faded jeans, the best dress code for a spanking. On my knees, you little macho cockteaser!" Daddy gripped Sonny's ass and slapped it firmly, giving him pleasure-pain, and Sonny moaned with joy. Noticing that his new son had a bulging crotch, Daddy caressed it eagerly, but he ordered, "Don't you think of cumming now, my little bastard. Keep your nectar for Daddy's insatiable mouth!"

Paul and Jeff quickly moved to the bedroom for a match of horny wrestling. They got naked in less than a minute and jumped in the ring for round one: massage. By experience, Paul knew that any massage is good for any man, gay or straight. A guy who has the opportunity to cum while someone else is doing the work always appreciates a set of helping hands.

Daddy oiled Sonny's body with a plan to wrestle with him, massage his round butt, squeeze his tight balls, and stroke his dynamic rod. He always liked to observe the reaction of a guy as he discreetly spread the legs and traveled up the thighs, working the upper leg muscles and nonchalantly touching the balls. Instant stiff reaction, instant throbbing cock! "With a thick pink dick like that," he said, "you are sent by God. You are my *god*son."

Jeff replied, "Your most obedient one, Holy Daddy! Can I lick your succulent mushroom?"

"Round two is about to start. It's called sixty-nine, but first we have to wrestle."

All oiled up, daddy and son went into a smaller room where there was not one single piece of furniture, just a rubber mat covering the whole floor. Paul ordered Jeff to join him, knowing well that any little whore acts like a bitch toward a man who shows an ounce of fucking affection. The pleasure in oil wrestling resides in the fact that the prized cock, balls, or ass always slides away, doubling the energy required of the wrestlers to finally grab the trophy.

When both men had reached the savage cock-sucking position in the wrestling match, it did not take Daddy too long to bring Sonny to the verge of a climax. He ordered him to explode in his mouth, eager as he was to taste 100 percent American honey. Daddy swallowed every drop, smiled in a victory gesture, and proudly heralded, "This milky nectar is divine, my goddamn little cowboy!"

Daddy was now ready for round three. He spit a little bit of son's sperm on his anus and started to lick the flowering rosebud in a frenzy, pushing his tongue as deep as possible, moaning with pleasure. Sonny had never experienced an ass-licking climax like that, so much that he exploded again.

There was no doubt that Daddy and Sonny, both mature men, had won their wrestling match, but the fun was not over. A hot shower proved to be another round of pleasure as Daddy directed the pointed water jet at Sonny's asshole, triggering another hard-on.

"Goddamn it, you are a fucking rutting stallion!" Daddy exclaimed.

Jeff replied, "Only because my mature and experienced daddy is insatiable."

A tale must have a happy ending. Let it be known that Paul and Jeff lived happily ever after ... or, as we read in *One Thousand and One Nights,* "happily until there came to them the one who destroys all happiness." In other words, death.

5.5　Chat Room Becomes a Sex Arena

enry joined an online gay dating site called Son Seeks Daddy, an ideal platform for someone whose libido seemed to increase after sixty-five. He had just turned seventy and had never felt so damn horny! In the middle of the night, somewhere between two and three o'clock, Henry would enter chat room three, for mature and younger members, and always find a potential son under fifty. The country of residence didn't really matter as long as the guy indicated "oral versatile" in his profile info. From Toronto, Canada, Henry was bilingual and liked to use his tongue for man-to-man pleasure—*plaisir homme-à-homme*.

The horny Canadian had barely entered chat room three when a certain William sent a chat request. Henry checked the guy's profile: forty-nine, five foot eleven, 187 pounds, from London (England), oral versatile, seeking a date between sixty and eighty. The pic gallery portrayed a handsome well-dressed Brit who looked like a lawyer or professor. No photo of his cock or ass—and no profile text either, which was kind of unusual. Pics of hard-ons and hungry butts were common on that dating site, but neither Henry nor William showcased their manhood in the public gallery. The private gallery was another story.

Henry offered three face pics, like William, and told potential sons that he was a full-time romantic writer looking for a man with whom he could first have a conversation, then cuddle, hug, and kiss. "I have a fetish for jockstraps, can give a spanking if you like that, especially if you wear tight blue jeans. I love the smell of virility; a clean but sweaty ass is the best perfume, drives me crazy. I enjoy oral sex, using my tongue in *every* way possible!"

That last sentence and the well-chosen face pics were probably what prompted William to say "Hi there, handsome!" Henry accepted, even if London, Ontario, would have been much closer than London, England. William was, in fact, American born and currently visiting an "enterprising" uncle in Boston, so not too far from Toronto.

William skipped the blah-blah-blah of introduction and went directly to the point: "I love a cut cock."

"Bingo! Mine is cut, perhaps smaller than yours, but has a cute pink mushroom," said Henry.

"Mmm, nice. Love cream of mushroom soup."

Henry asked, "Do you sometimes come to Toronto?"

"Would like to cum there," replied William.

"Would love to eat your ass."

"You are more than welcome."

"Do you like to wear jockstraps?" inquired Henry.

"Love them!"

Henry explained why jocks were his big fetish, which started when he was in boarding school and played hockey. The coach had explained that the cup of a jockstrap would protect his genitals from a flying puck. Seeing other guys put on jocks always made Henry feel nicely weird, if not to say queer. It was only years later that he discovered the erotic side of this male garment, which came in various colors. "The jockstrap wraps the balls nicely," he wrote to William. "It's an invitation to squeeze them."

"Squeeze mine really hard, honey."

"It frames the ass perfectly for a spanking."

William replied, "I need a good one, Daddy."

"And a jock holds one's dick in place for a nice bite—until it pops out of the elastic, ready to be sucked."

"Right on! We each wear a jockstrap, different color, and suck each other off. I want you to cream my face!"

Henry could hear William moaning, so he took the opportunity to go one step further. The Canadian was so hungry that he could eat the Brit's asshole for breakfast, lunch, dinner, and a midnight snack. The sentence in Henry's profile text—"I enjoy oral sex, using my tongue in *every* way possible"—was an understatement. "You know, William, I find a clean but sweaty ass so fucking tasty."

"Me too," replied William. "A smelly and musky hole is divine—the *nec plus ultra* in sniffing."

"Sometimes I put whipped cream on my partner's rosebud. Yummy!" said Henry.

William said, "Mmm, push some inside my shit hole."

"Tongue-twisting my way into your satanic haven would be heaven on earth!"

William sent a pic of his smooth, wide, firm ass to Henry. It obviously wasn't a selfie, because William was bending over, legs wide apart to show a rosebud the size of a tulip bud. The photographer was probably the American uncle.

Whoever took the photo, the result was awesome and made Henry cry out loud, "*Fuck!* Your ass is a full-course meal."

"That's exactly what my uncle keeps saying," said William.

"Your profile indicates a preference for men between sixty and eighty," said Henry. "I want someone younger than me, like a dude your age."

"Good to hear. I've always gone with men older than me, much older."

"If we met, would you want to fuck me?"

William said, "Sorry, I'm a bottom."

"I could finger-fuck you," Henry said.

"Push as many fingers in my butt's hungry mouth as you can, Daddy!"

"Have you ever been fist-fucked? Not that I'm experienced, but I could learn quickly."

William said, "I'd love you to fist me."

"Strange how a shit hole can be so energizing and fucking gorgeous," Henry said. "When I was a teenager and someone called me *asshole*, I had no idea it was a compliment, lol. I only discovered my attraction to guys when I was around twenty-two."

"I was seduced by an older guy when I was much younger—around fourteen, I guess," said William.

"I studied at a seminary, but no luck for me, lol. One kid got expelled in the middle of the night because he had been caught in bed with another student."

"I had a very dominant professor in his seventies when I went to college. Alleluia!"

Henry explained that his first gay sex experience was with a young prostitute, and that he had almost gone to jail when the police discovered what they had called the homosexual vice ring. William and Henry shared a common "inexperience"—they had never been with a woman and never seen a cunt.

The Canadian suspected that the Brit, like himself, had probably never experienced something that turned Henry on. "I'm not into golden showers myself, but I jerk off looking at a video where two young dudes piss and drink, piss on asshole and rim. Fuck! They give me a boner."

William replied, "I'd love to swallow your amber champagne."

"You mean I could pee in your mouth?" asked Henry.

"Mmm. Fuck yeah!"

"Don't leave Boston. There's a direct Porter flight from Toronto. I want to come over immediately, because you are so amazingly hot!"

Henry and William's chat lasted over an hour. They never met face-to-face, but they both creamed their jockstraps with fingers in their assholes.

6

Bondage and Group Sex

6.1 Personal Service Guaranteed

Harry travels to give conferences of a historic nature, such as fifty years of gay liberation in Canada and the United States. He lives in Toronto and is invited to an international LGBT summit in Montréal. His motto is "Treat yourself. You're worth it." When he travels, Harry takes the VIA train in business class. The preboarding priority, extra leg room (he's six foot three), meal, and open bar justify the increased cost.

The train leaves Union Station on time, at exactly 11:45 a.m. The employee checking the tickets is a tall, handsome black guy in his late twenties. Harry finds out that Jonathan is originally from St. Martin in the Caribbean Islands and that his title is personal service attendant (PSA). *How personal will he get?* That's the question on Harry's mind. Since there are few clients in business class, Jonathan has free time to chat with everyone, but he seems more interested in Harry. They first exchange smiles, and then Jonathan asks if he can sit with Harry during his short break between two station stops.

Harry immediately thinks this PSA is making a move. He feels Jonathan's knee pressing his thigh as though by accident when the train jolts—or is it intentional? At the first station stop, most of the other business-class travelers disembark, and no one gets on. Now there are only two clients in VIA 1: Harry and a little old lady sitting farther back. Jonathan invites Harry to take a place in the two-seat section near the kitchenette. "We can have more privacy," he adds.

As soon as they are comfortably installed, Harry feels a wandering hand on his thigh, triggering a bulge in his crotch. Jonathan caresses this offering with one hand and unzips his own trousers with the other. He is wearing no underwear, and his bazooka is peeking out. The sight of this black manhood arouses Harry, who dares to kiss the handsome PSA on the lips.

"White lips, cock, and ass drive me crazy," Jonathan whispers.

"Black guys have the same effect on me."

"There are no clients coming on board for fifty-five minutes, so we can have some fun."

"Wow!" exclaims Harry. "I guess VIA means having a very important attendant."

Jonathan says, "Exactly. You'll get first-class treatment starting with this joystick—or should I say, dark chocolate bar?"

"A real Toblerone, my friend!" Harry kneels and starts caressing the thick dick and sucking the hard rod.

Jonathan wants his share of goods and invites Harry to follow him into the men's washroom. As soon as they're behind a locked door, they embrace feverishly, drop their trousers, squeeze each other's buns, and frot their cocks.

Harry tickles his partner's crack, triggering a moan of pleasure. "I want to eat your black ass, my prized TSH," he says.

"What does TSH stand for?" asks Jonathan.

"Tall, slim, and handsome."

"Thanks! My butthole is all yours."

Harry loses no time in burying his face in Jonathan's crack, licking it, spanking his cheeks, sucking his rosebud, and tongue-twisting his way in this satanic haven. The train jolts now and then, which helps Harry to dart the chocolate butthole more wildly.

Jonathan's dick is now seven inches long and more than ready for action. He's excited by Harry's hairy ass and anus. Soap is the only lubricant on hand, so Jonathan shoves a clean weapon in Harry's tight asshole, making him almost cry. "I've never had such a big hold-up. You're hurting me, but it's a thrilling pain in the ass."

The train is moving at a steady pace and the coach seems like it's wagging its tail. Jonathan follows the rhythm and pounds his client, but refrains from exploding. He slaps Harry's butt firmly and makes him moan with pleasure.

The supervisor of passenger services happens to walk by the washroom and wonders what's going on. He knocks on the door and asks, "Is everything okay there?"

"Yes, it's fine, thank you. Don't worry, I'm in good hands ... I mean, in a good ... position."

The supervisor is not sure—or is intrigued by the hot moans—so he uses his key to open the door. What he sees is a spectacle, an invitation to join in the hot action. The threesome encounter cannot last too long, however, because a new VIA 1 passenger is boarding at the next stop.

The older lady disembarks, and an athletic guy wearing Speedos sits in the middle of the coach, taking care to flaunt his manhood. Harry, Jonathan, and the supervisor smile lusciously. There is no place in the bathroom for a foursome orgy, but the entire coach can easily become the theater of hot role-playing. Act 2 is about to unfold, and the actors are in a deck of cards: blackjack, king of spades, ace of ass, queen of cock. Heart trump, obviously.

6.2 Bound to Please His Master

O rvo had always been called a nerd, mainly because of his slim frame, boyish face, and glasses. Even at university, he did not generally fit into the mainstream of the prevalent culture. Orvo's classmates ignored that his fetishes included bondage, foul body odors, humiliation role play, and other kinky practices. The nerd had always been good with ropes, because he secretly practiced self-bondage alone in his bedroom. Gags were also a big thing for him, especially using dirty socks. And he liked wearing sports gear—the look and feel of tight football uniforms while tied up aroused him. He made videos of himself, disguising his face in a leather mask.

For his twentieth birthday, Orvo dreamed of exploring his bondage fantasy with an older guy, but his timid nature held him back. Then he met a fit blue-collar guy who came over to build a garden box for the backyard. Halfway through the job, the stud was perspiring, covered in grime and sawdust. Every time the construction guy bent down, Orvo could see a red jockstrap waistband.

Only gay guys wear those, he thought. *Now is my chance!* Alone in the house, Orvo decided to play it cool. He had a plan …

"Would you like a beer?"

"That'd be great, thanks. I'm Paul. What's your name?"

"Orvo, but you can call me Orja."

Paul asked, "You mean like *slave*?"

"Yeah, it's just a fantasy."

Paul smiled, took a big sip of beer, removed his shirt, returned to work, and quickly finished the job. He, too, had a plan. As soon as he closed his toolbox, he asked Orvo if it was possible to take a quick shower.

"Of course," replied the young man. "You can undress in my bedroom, which is next to the bathroom."

While Paul was showering, Orvo noticed that on the bed—in addition to a pair of jeans, a dirty T-shirt, a jockstrap, and smelly socks—was a long rope. He grabbed it and circled his waist, moaning with pleasure, not noticing that Paul had come out of the bathroom and was watching him.

Paul said, "I left it on the bed for you, Orja."

"Oh, you surprised me."

"In a lustful way, I'm sure. Can I undress you?"

"Please do, and tie me up too," said Orja.

"Don't worry," said Paul. "I'm kinky too, and bondage is my thing—but I'm the master."

"And me, your obedient Orja!"

There was no four-poster bed to use for restraining Orja's ankles and wrists, but an armchair was second best. Paul ordered his slave to undress and sit at a ninety-degree angle. He bound his wrists to the armrests and his ankles to the legs of the chair. Then the master paused, put on his red jockstrap, and whispered in Orja's ear, "The best is yet to come, my little slut!"

Retrieving his toolbox, Paul pulled out some electrical wire that he used to make a cock ring, giving Orja an immediate erection. Then Paul squeezed his slave's balls and tied them separately with wire, triggering moans of pleasure.

"This is the best birthday party I've ever had, sir!" exclaimed Orja.

"Fine, but we need to put cream on the cake."

"Do you mean one hundred percent homo nectar?"

Paul said, "Of course, you fucking orja. I'm going to suck you with frenzy and jerk you off to cream my face!"

When Paul saw how obedient and horny Orja was, it was time for the next step. He liberated his slave from the chair and ordered him to get dressed and follow the guide to man-to-man pleasure. They climbed into Paul's truck and drove to a secluded barn where Orja was again tied up, this time on an X-shaped cross with foot rests. The rope swirled around his ankles and up to his wrists, giving Paul full access to a round, firm young ass.

Paul's rod was now hard and ready to pump, but he followed his introductory ritual, caressing Orja's butt firmly and then slapping it vigorously and triggering moans of pleasure. That was the signal for Paul's oral attack. He bit the succulent buns, licked the crack, and darted his tongue inside to reach the anus, which he chewed and sucked to the rhythm of Orja's cries of joy.

"The best is yet to come, my fucking little slave!" Paul opened the Crisco can and lubricated his hard dick, shoved his rod in Orja's asshole, and started pounding until he exploded his own 100 percent homo nectar.

Orja was no longer a virgin. He had entered manhood with brilliant colors!

6.3   On the Altar of Masculinity

Every day after lunch, Paul drops by his ex-lover's town house to walk Lilly, who's half Chihuahua, half Pomeranian. Usually he just goes for a stroll in the nearby park, sits on the bench with Lilly on his knees, and watches other dog owners on the leash. After all, man's best friend is the leader!

Today Paul decides to walk toward the National Ballet School in Toronto, Canada. Lilly enjoys sniffing a new sidewalk trail, and Paul takes pleasure in admiring athletic guys going in and out of the ballet school. Just as he's about to head back home, Paul notices a man who looks about thirty, with a short beard and mustache, running past him. When the man reaches the entrance to the building, he disappears behind the revolving doors.

As a writer always in search of characters for his short stories, Paul immediately memorizes the look of this athletic man. The beard and mustache highlight an attractive angel face, giving it a little demon glow. What could be the name of this handsome dude? Certainly not

John, Peter, or Bob. Probably something like Oscar, Julius, or Mathew. Paul opts for the latter and starts imagining what Mathew's clothes are like.

Mathew is wearing a short-sleeved, green-and-purple plaid shirt. His tight black leggings firmly wrap his round butt and enhance his muscular thighs. Strangely, the leggings have a large hole on the left knee, which gives Mathew a macho look and triggers Paul's imagination. He imagines Mathew as a ballet teacher or coach.

Mathew is a visiting choreographer from Birmingham, England. His job is to produce a performance with seven male students, titled *On the Altar of Masculinity*. The seven dancers do not have a written script; instead, they follow Mathew's directions.

First he says, "Remove your clothes, and just keep your jockstraps on." Six dancers bear the colors of the rainbow flag: red, orange, yellow, green, blue, and violet. The seventh dancer wears a white jockstrap.

Mathew quickly notices that the white pouch is slowly but surely bulging. He gives this student the name Virile and orders the rainbow dancers to surround him, lift him into a horizontal position, rest his body on their shoulders, and march toward a dark oak dining table to the music of "The Little Drummer Boy."

"Slide Virile onto the center of the table, while caressing every inch of his body."

Immediately the thick hard rod stretches the white jockstrap to a point where the mushroom proudly sneaks out. The spotlight enhances this majestic protuberance. Mathew can't help caressing his own stiff cock, and he sees that Virile's asset has triggered each colored jockstrap to bulge in harmony, in gay pride.

Mathew had expected this, and he can now give a name to each of the six proud young bearers. The red jockstrap is called Mars, orange is Jupiter, yellow is Neptune, green is Apollo, blue is Vulcan, and violet is Mercury. The six Greek gods are now aligned to lustfully honor Virile on the altar of masculinity.

Like the red eyes of "Tyger Tyger, burning bright in the forests of the night," by William Blake, Mars approaches Virile and embraces him passionately. He is followed by Jupiter, who takes on a French accent to give a penetrating French kiss to the graceful ballet dancer in his white jockstrap. The yellow Neptune has no choice but to offer a golden shower and pee on Virile's pecs, shoulders, and chin, and even in his mouth. The green Apollo has to be true to his python symbol, so he avidly sucks Virile's golden rod. The blue Vulcan uses his hand like a hammer to spank Virile's round and firm butt. The violet Mercury, god of communication, can use only his linguistic skills, so he plunges his sharp tongue into Virile's sweaty rosebud.

Mathew has kept for himself the climax step of his choreography. He strips naked, lubricates his engine, and starts pounding Virile's fucking asshole with intensity. In no time, six candlesticks glow on the altar of masculinity. Virile has now become Zeus, and it is a duty, an honor, to make each of his gods explode and reap the reward of swallowing their creamy nectar.

6.4 Two Men and a Truck

George had always saved for a private pension plan and was able to take Freedom 55. He sold his house at a profit and bought a condo in downtown Toronto. There were many moving companies, but the choice seemed obvious: Two Men and a Truck. It sounded like an adventurous invitation with daredevil innuendoes.

The two men were called John and Jim. Both were in their midthirties, and both were muscular and handsome, of medium build. John had an anchor tattooed on his left arm, and Jim had a short dark beard that gave him a macho look. They emptied the house in just over two hours. George watched them eagerly, especially when they bent to lift a sofa or bookcase, showing firm, round asses in tight jeans. He offered them a Coke or a beer, which they accepted with a smile.

The last item packed was a six-foot painting of a nude black guy hung like a stallion. John whispered to Jim, "I think this guy is gay, so maybe we're in for a bit of fun!"

At the condo, George directed the movers to the right

rooms, asking them to place each piece of furniture in the proper position. The tall painting was the last thing to be unwrapped, and it had the power to attract the attention of anyone in the room.

"We can hang it for you. Where does it go?" Jim asked.

"In the living room, between the two windows."

John asked, "Is he someone you know?"

"Yeah, it's the self-portrait of a close friend."

"Are you hung like him?" joked Jim.

"No, but I think you both have hot rods that need attention. Am I right?"

"Can we take a shower first?" asked John.

Not waiting for an answer, Jim and John removed their sweaty shirts, revealing sizzling six-packs. When they bent down to untie their boots, George grabbed their asses and slapped them, triggering moans of satisfaction. The shower area was big enough for three guys ready to hug. George soaped his movers' hard dicks, rinsed them clean, licked them avidly, and started to suck each one eagerly.

John's boner was thick, cut, with a bursting mushroom fueled by nuts in a tight bag. Jim's chopper was a slender, uncut dipstick attached to low-hanging balls. He tried to reach for George's cute curved piece of meat, saying that they also wanted a share of the meal. John suggested, "Let's go in the bedroom, where the king-size bed is a good arena for a virile combat."

George, John, and Jim took their places on the mattress, forming a circle, each with a dork in his mouth. You could have called it the sixth Olympic circle. The position was ideal to easily switch from sixty-nine to ass-rimming, an exercise that generated a fanfare of "Fucking awesome!"

John and Jim had made their plan on the way from the house to the condo. They were hired to move furniture, but why could this job not have fringe benefits, as was often the case? They saw the good-looking George as the ideal recipient for their masculine nectar, each positioned at a different entry port, each ready to explode at the same time.

With only spit on his seven-and-a-half-inch pistol, Jim started pushing it slowly into George's tight ass. Soon the entire length was deep inside. Then Jim slid his hands under George's ass, lifted him, pulled his cock almost entirely out, and let George fall back down on it and impale himself. George moaned louder.

John was not the type of guy to remain on the sidelines. He shoved his thick manhood back and forth in George's mouth. His intention wasn't to face-fuck the more-than-willing client, but to literally skull-fuck him. He kept yelling, "Take it all, my little whore. You're going to love my cum flavor in your mouth, you sweet son of bitch!"

George had no idea that double dipping could be so fucking tasty.

Feeling their orgasms building with every thrust, John and Jim couldn't refrain from commenting on this man-to-man pleasure. "Gosh, my girlfriend isn't half the fuck you are!" John exclaimed.

To the tune of this compliment, George began to stroke his own cock, bringing it to a climax. In harmony, all three men opened fire at the same time—one in a hungry ass, one in a warm mouth, one on his hairy chest.

When the movers left the condo, they wondered if they should hire George as a manager and change the name of the company to Three Men and a Hot Truck.

6.5 Locker Room Foursome

Twice a week, four friends—Ted, Jim, Henry, and Mike, all in their late twenties—meet at the community gym for cardio exercise and indoor track running before playing racquetball, tennis, or squash. Ted and Henry like to wear black shorts over their bulging white jockstraps, and Jim and Mike prefer Fastskin Speedos that enhance their manhoods.

Today Ted and Jim played tennis against Henry and Mike, ending up losing 7–5 and 6–4. Jim is a sore loser and was pretty aggressive when they all entered the locker room. "Why can't you move your fucking ass, Ted? You have to learn how to play with me, damn it!" Ted just smiled, thinking of the various ways he could play with the most handsome guy of the foursome.

Jim took off his T-shirt, threw it into a locker, pulled out a towel, and started to whip Ted's ass, which offered no resistance. This triggered him to press his partner with one hand against the next locker and punch his firm round butt with the other hand. Ted now had a grin on his face. Jim could even hear him moan, so he got closer to bite his earlobe.

As they were getting undressed, Henry and Mike watched this sensuous confrontation. Getting a hard-on, Mike first tried to cover it with his towel, but seeing that Henry was discreetly massaging his genitals snugged in his sweaty jockstrap, he approached him and lowered the towel to reveal a fully erect cock. Unable to resist the divine offering, Henry started to suck his partner's bazooka.

By that time, Jim had pulled down Ted's shorts and kissed his rear end, and now he was licking his full jockstrap. He had also removed his Speedo, revealing a hot trouser snake that he whanged in Ted's crack. Jim was not ready to engulf his weapon, because he first wanted to get Ted's asshole moist and wet. No need to use a gel when you have a luscious wet tongue.

Rimming is often the first step to fucking, because it sexually stimulates the person who is to be penetrated. According to Gay Demon's dictionary, rimming can be done in homosexual, heterosexual, or bisexual relations. In porn, however, it is most often referred to as a gay sex practice.

Ted's ass is completely hairless, and his anus is amber, like the gemstone. Its natural beauty attracts Jim, who executes a full tongue-length inside swirl. He then pulls his partner's balls down near the anus and licks from the asshole to the testicles and back a few times. Jim's next step consists of pulling Ted's cock down and licking from the anus up to the balls, over and around the head of the dick, and back down again to the rosebud.

By now, Mike's dick is fully lubricated and rhythmically pounding Henry's back door, which is nicely framed by the jockstrap elastics. This sport attire has the advantage among many gay men of stimulating their libidos. A jockstrap is also an invitation to slap your partner's butt and squeeze his nicely wrapped balls. But why have duo fun when you can have foursome pleasure?

Ted and Jim, who were already sucking each other in an athletic sixty-nine choreography, joined Mike and Henry on the large locker room bench. It was almost a contest of who would suck the biggest engine, who would rim the tastiest arsehole, who would fuck the tightest buttocks.

Mike's pulsing shaft wasted no time in satisfying Ted's hungry asshole. "Since the day I met you, I've been dreaming of fucking your appetizing butt. My mighty pistol can now shoot a full load of ammunition in your faggot bumhole!"

As for Henry, he just wanted to suck Jim's meat thermometer and taste his milky nectar. "Every time I see you in the shower, I wonder how thrilling it would be to have your pecker grow and explode in my mouth. Now is my chance to transform fiction into reality. Fuck my mouth, pound my skull, and give it to me, because I badly need your hot lunch!"

When four horny guys meet in the arena of male pleasure, there is no limit to their performance. In the case of this virile scenario, not one tender word was exchanged. There was no place for emotions—just raw pleasure. No sweet kiss on the lips or caressing hand on the face. Again, just brutal satisfaction. A man's world can be a gay demon's haven or heaven.

6.6   Jeans, Brief, and Jockstrap Fantasies

Bruce and Jed, eighteen years old, were close friends—best friends, to be exact. But they had never shared a secret fantasy, not until a Friday afternoon that would change their lives. Bruce's parents had left for the long weekend, not knowing that they were giving their son a golden opportunity. He had hurried home after school, not noticing that Jed was following him at distance.

Bruce rushed upstairs to his bedroom without locking the front door and quickly changed clothes, choosing briefs one size too small and skin-tight jeans. The briefs molded his manhood perfectly, and the feel of thin faded denim always gave him a hard-on. Bruce took a hit of popper and started turning the pages of a gay jack-off magazine hidden under his mattress. The first pictures showed cute college guys in their underpants fondling their jockey pouches. The areas around their erect penises were soaked. They had obviously just ejaculated into their briefs.

By now, Jed had sneaked into the house and tiptoed

upstairs to his best friend's room. The door was half open, so he could hear Bruce moaning while masturbating through what he called sex jeans. "May I join in?" Jed asked.

Bruce turned around to see his best friend standing behind him, rubbing his own sizable bulge in tight denim. "I can't believe it, Jed. We're into the same things."

"What things, Bruce?"

"Well, the porn pictures are about guys in briefs and jeans, just like the ones we have on."

"You're right, Bruce. You know, when I wear them like this, I can shoot two or three times a day."

"I guess we're both queer for boys, queer for underpants, and queer for tight denim," said Bruce.

Jed said, "It's weird that there are two of us that way, and that we're best friends."

"Hey, buddy, if we weren't queer, we wouldn't be best friends," Bruce said.

Jed was a slim Irish lad with red hair, blue eyes, a freckled face, and a trim physique. Bruce, too, was well-built, dark blond, with a peaches-and-cream complexion. Wearing tight Levi's was the discovery of their adolescence.

"Oh, Jed, feeling the underpants rubbing my cock and balls against the denim is always an invitation to jack off."

"Yeah, the feeling is so intense that I can explode without a helping hand."

"I'm sure you won't mind rubbing crotches with your best friend, right?" Bruce said.

Bruce invited Jed to join him on the patio and climb into a large Jacuzzi. They immediately felt the bubbles tickle their balls and stiff dicks. They embraced in a luscious groin massage, their weapons trying to poke holes through the thin denim. Jed suggested that it would be nice to have a closer look—in bed. They reluctantly removed their sex jeans and positioned themselves for sixty-nine underpants choreography. To add spice, Bruce switched his brief for a jockstrap. Another hit of popper and Ted was rimming his partner's rosebud, tongue-fucking him with frenzy. Bruce was eating his friend's crotch, feeling the hard cannon leaking into his briefs. This and Ted's twisting tongue made him explode in a sweaty jock pouch.

The next day, Ted and Bruce headed for a male-porn movie arcade. As they walked past the maze of cubicles, they noticed a kid hanging out next to an open door. The second time around, Bruce felt a hand squeeze his bulge and Ted felt a firm hand on his sex jeans. An invitation for a threesome could not be more direct. More surprisingly, the kid was a schoolmate called Doug.

"We heard that you like to hang around the locker room and bury your face in the jockstrap bin," said Ted.

"Hmm, yeah!" said Doug. "Guys' briefs and cum in Levi's also turn me on."

Bruce said, "I guess the three of us all enjoy the same

fantasies. Care to join us at my place? My parents are gone for the long weekend."

"Sure, if you can guarantee me boy-to-boy pleasure," Doug replied.

"Don't worry, you're in for a treat!" Bruce assured him.

When Doug took off his jeans, he was wearing a Bike Athletic jockstrap, which landed in Bruce's face and triggered a delicious jerk. Ted grabbed the kid's round ass and started to push his tongue into the succulent fuck hole. It didn't take long before Doug gave a stifled "*Fuck*" and Bruce felt the jock-pouch filing with jism. The two best friends immediately creamed their sex jeans. Feeling a guy's jockstrap, brief, and skin-tight jeans drove all three of them wild.

But the best was to come on the holiday Monday. Doug revealed that two guys from the football team were always parading in the locker room, exhibiting their bulging jockstraps and slapping each other's butt. There was no doubt in his mind that all the ingredients were present for a great orgy ...

6.7 GAY Olympic Games

n 2025, Canada, the United States, Australia, Great Britain, Norway, Sweden, Denmark, the Netherlands, Argentina, and other countries each had a Golden Army of Youth (GAY) composed of athletic college guys between the ages of eighteen and twenty. Members were recruited to offer support to the military when it was called upon to rescue people after a natural disaster such as a tornado, tsunami, flood, avalanche, or forest fire.

In each country, GAY members trained regularly to be in good shape. This included a one-hour jogging session in the morning, followed by gym exercises, a team sport challenge such as soccer or hockey in the afternoon, and boxing or wrestling matches in the evening. The result was astonishing: an elite squad of robust young men who would have won any Mr. Muscle championship or Best Fit contest, not to mention a Well-Endowed competition.

The coach of Sweden's Golden Army of Youth woke up one morning with an idea. We are going to hold the first GAY Olympic Games. Bjorn Andersson was a respected, handsome, and virile homosexual who got what he wanted nine out of ten times. One exception was that he had never fucked the commanding officer of the National Home Guard, who nevertheless wholeheartedly supported Bjorn's initiative. For the first GAY Olympic Games, four disciplines were selected: longest erection, thickest cock, sperm throw, and longest fucking orgasm. "In any of these sports," insisted Bjorn, "there can be cheerleaders or helping hands and mouths, and sex partners can be either male or female."

Members of the Golden Army of Youth were healthy normal guys, not circus freaks. The five guys registered in the longest erection discipline didn't compare to Jonah Falcon, the American actor reported as having the world's largest penis at 9.5 inches in length when flaccid and 13.5 inches when erect. And then there was Roberto Esquivel Cabrera from Mexico, who claimed to have a cock measuring a whopping 18 inches. That wasn't an official record, however, because it was believed that Cabrera stretched his weapon abnormally with weights and refused to remove the bandages around his bazooka for proper measurement.

The five countries competing for the longest erection were Australia, the United States, Argentina, Norway, and Denmark. The cheerleaders were male and female strippers who were allowed to suck or jerk on demand. Oral and manual stimulation couldn't last more than ninety seconds, and judges monitored this closely. Three guys and two girls gave helping hands and mouths, and Bjorn wasn't surprised when the results were announced.

Erick Olsen, from Norway, with the help of Christian Greasy Hand, reached 11.89 inches and won the bronze medal. Timothy Conway, from the USA, with the help of Danny Luscious Tongue, reached 11.95 inches and won the silver medal. Jeff Smith, from Australia, with the help of Larry Hot Lips, reached 12 inches and won the gold medal. Bjorn Andersson concluded that these results confirmed the old saying that boys will be boys—or that real boys have more fun with real boys.

The rules for the thickest cock discipline were simple and involved no touching at all. The competitors had to put their hands behind their backs, concentrate on some kind of stimulation to get an erection, and let the judges measure the girth or circumference of their appendages. An international study by the *British Journal of Urology* measured the penises of 15,521 men, and from their findings, the average flaccid girth was 3 inches, and erect penises averaged 4 inches. For size reference, that's about the width of a tube of toothpaste.

Joseph Dufour from Canada, Luis Gerissimo from Argentina, and Liam Nilsson from Sweden were the three laureates in that competition. To get aroused, Joseph invited a guy to put his asshole almost in Joseph's face; he measured 4.04 inches and won the bronze medal. Luis called upon an athletic dude to fuck a twink in a jockstrap; he measured 4.09 inches and won the silver medal. Liam asked two male cheerleaders to take a golden shower; he measured a whopping 4.2 inches and won the gold medal. Again, an all-boys cast.

The sperm throw competition was about masturbating and ejaculating as far as possible. Semen exits the penis at an average speed of 16.9 miles per hour. So what's the farthest distance a man can ejaculate? Your answer has to be reasonable. I don't accept something like "thirty yards out my window, flew into someone else's window, nailed my sixty-year-old neighbor in the eye, and he died of a concussion." Wikipedia tells us that Horst Schultz achieved 19.6 feet! His ejaculation speed was 41.99 miles per hour. That should qualify as an extreme sport, don't you think?

Putting quantity aside, some men can ejaculate up to 3 feet. Don't worry, however, if you feel your own ejaculate isn't going the distance. The average distance for a male ejaculation is 6.69 to 9.84 inches. Oscar Christensen from Denmark, Lars De Jong from the Netherlands, and Timothy Conway from the USA were the three laureates in this competition. They were allowed to call upon almost any kind of support.

Oscar asked a hairy bear cheerleader to plunge a dildo back and forth in his rear end, and he reached 9.05 inches, winning the bronze medal. Lars asked a soccer player in a bulging jockstrap to play with his nipples, and he reached 10.23 inches, winning the silver medal. Timothy asked Bjorn Andersson to suck his asshole with frenzy, and he reached 11.02 inches, winning the gold medal. It seems that male support brings the best results in these GAY Olympic Games!

For the longest fucking orgasm competition, the rule is simple—you can penetrate only one partner, male or female. The average time before orgasm is about six minutes, and most men last between four and eleven minutes; anyone who lasts longer than twenty minutes is considered an outlier. Not surprisingly, all three finalists chose to fuck a young man's tight ass. The British prime minister's son won the bronze medal with fourteen minutes, the Canadian prime minister's son won the silver medal with sixteen minutes, and the Argentinian president's son won the gold medal with eighteen minutes.

Bjorn Andersson was warmly applauded for having organized the first GAY Olympic Games. His unexpected reward was having the opportunity to rim Timothy's rosebud and simultaneously reach his own orgasm.

About the Author

Paul-François Sylvestre is a gay, French-Canadian author. His double minority status has led him to write twenty-four essays, ten novels, three collections of short stories, two books of poetry, two collections of Christmas tales, and a biography of his twin sister—all in French. Mr. Sylvestre's first book was a diary of his coming out in his early twenties. He wrote the history of the Canadian Gay Liberation Movement, which started in 1969.

Mr. Sylvestre is the book critic for Toronto's French-language weekly paper L'Express and for the literary blog www.jaipourmonlire.ca. His English-language texts are recent and are all gay porn stories, the vast majority of them included in this book. He is a regular contributor to the Swedish site Gay Demon.

Printed in the United States
By Bookmasters